Sarah's World is Crumbling

"What are those?"

"Just some flyers I got from the doctor," said Mrs. Gordon, "nothing interesting."

"All right, what's wrong, Mom? You're not just feeling tired, are you?"

Mrs. Gordon sighed, and glanced at the pamphlets. "Sarah, the truth is I don't know what's wrong. I went to the doctor a few days ago for some routine tests, and they found something surprising—"

"What do they think it might be?" asked Sarah. Her heart began beating in her chest when Mrs. Gordon asked her to close the door. She was worried for her mother, and a little unnerved that she was carrying such a big secret.

18 Pine St.

Taking Sides

Written by
Stacie Johnson

Created by
WALTER DEAN MYERS

A Seth Godin Production

BANTAM BOOKS

NEW YORK · TORONTO · LONDON · SYDNEY · AUCKLAND

RL 5, age 10 and up

TAKING SIDES
A Bantam Book / September 1994

*Thanks to Susan Korman, Amy Berkower, Fran Lebowitz, Marva Martin,
Michael Cader, Megan O'Connor, José Arroyo, Julie Maner, Chris Angelilli,
Martin Erb, Karen Watts, Ellen Kenny, Helene, Alex and Lucy Wood.*

18 Pine St. is a trademark of Seth Godin Productions, Inc.

ISBN 0-553-56564-8

Published simultaneously in the United States and Canada

Bantam Books are published by Bantam Books, a division of Bantam Doubleday
Dell Publishing Group, Inc. Its trademark, consisting of the words "Bantam
Books" and the portrayal of a rooster, is Registered in U.S. Patent and
Trademark Office and in other countries. Marca Registrada. Bantam Books, 1540
Broadway, New York, New York 10036.

PRINTED IN THE UNITED STATES OF AMERICA

OPM 0 9 8 7 6 5 4 3 2 1

For Patty Jo

18 Pine St.

There is a card shop at 8 Pine St., and a shop that sells sewing supplies at 10 Pine that's only open in the afternoons and on Saturdays if it doesn't rain. For some reason that no one seems to know or care about, there is no 12, 14, or 16 Pine. The name of the pizzeria at 18 Pine St. was Antonio's before Mr. and Mrs. Harris took it over. Mr. Harris removed Antonio's sign and just put up a sign announcing the address. By the time he got around to thinking of a name for the place, everybody was calling it 18 Pine.

The Crew at 18 Pine St.

Sarah Gordon is the heart and soul of the group. Sarah's pretty, with a great smile and a warm, caring attitude that makes her a terrific friend. Sarah's the reason that everyone shows up at 18 Pine St.

Tasha Gordon, tall, sexy, and smart, is Sarah's cousin. Since her parents died four years ago, Tasha has moved from relative to relative. Now she's living with Sarah and her family—maybe for good.

Cindy Phillips is Sarah's best friend. Cindy is petite, with dark, radiant skin and a cute nose. She wears her black hair in braids. Cindy's been Sarah's neighbor and friend since she moved from Jamaica when she was three.

Kwame Brown's only a sophomore, but that doesn't stop him from being part of the crew. As the smartest kid in the group, he's the one Jennifer turns to for help with her homework.

Jennifer Wilson is the poor little rich girl. Her parents are divorced, and all the charge cards and clothes in the world can't make up for it. Jennifer's tall and thin, with cocoa-colored skin and a body that's made for all those designer clothes she wears.

April Winter has been to ten schools in the last ten years—and she hopes she's at Murphy to stay. Her energy, blond hair, and offbeat personality make her a standout at school.

And there's Dave Hunter, Brian Wu, and the rest of the gang. You'll meet them all in the halls of Murphy High and after school for a pizza at 18 Pine St.

One

The Mad Soaper had struck again.

When Sarah Gordon and her friends Cindy Phillips and Kwame Brown walked into the Murphy High cafeteria, they immediately saw the graffiti scrawled in white soap on the picture window that looked out onto the courtyard. The graffiti artist had drawn a picture of Wally the goat, the school's mascot. Underneath, in large block letters, was written "Murphy Rools!"

"He didn't even spell it right," Cindy said, pointing to the window.

"Hold on, how do you know it's a 'he'?" Kwame said. He looked at Cindy over his black-rimmed glasses. "It could be a 'she.'"

"How many girls do you know who go around writing graffiti?" said Sarah, answering for her best friend.

"And besides," Cindy added with a smile, "a girl

would know how to spell 'rules'!"

Kwame followed his friends to the hot lunch line. "Maybe that's why she hasn't been caught yet," he persisted. "If the teachers at Murphy are looking for a boy who can't spell, she's home free."

Leave it to Kwame to come up with a logical answer, Sarah thought. Even though he was only a sophomore—a year younger than Sarah and Cindy—Kwame was one of Murphy High's brightest students.

"All right, you three," said Robert Thornton as he approached them. "Open your book bags. This is a soap bust!" His handsome brown-skinned face was set in a mock frown.

"You first," Cindy replied. "This soaping thing is something you would do."

Robert grinned and shook his head as he picked up a cafeteria tray. "Not my handwriting," he said. "But I've got to hand it to whoever it is. He's been at it for a month, and he hasn't been caught yet."

Sarah looked at the letters smeared on the glass. The first message had appeared in late February, just the word "Murphy" written over dozens of lockers. A week later, a caricature of Wally had appeared on a wall in the school's pool room. Since then, there were few open spaces the graffiti artist had left untouched. Mr. Schlesinger, the vice principal, had called on the students to tell him who was vandalizing school property. But so far no one had come forward.

"I still think it's a she," Kwame murmured.

Dave Hunter smiled at Sarah as he placed his lunch

tray next to hers. The Hunters lived across the street from the Gordons, and Sarah had known Dave since grade school, long before he had shot up to over six feet and become a star on the Murphy High basketball team. She didn't remember when she had discovered she was attracted to him; she was just glad he had made the same discovery about her.

"Halfway through the day," Dave declared, "and the worst is over. That math test did me in."

"It was a killer," Robert agreed. He imitated the voice of a television news reporter. "I'm live at the Murphy lunchroom, speaking to a survivor of Mr. Cala's math test." He placed his fork under Dave's chin as if it were a microphone. "Can you describe how you feel, sir?"

"Lucky to be alive, man," said Dave, his lips trembling. Everyone laughed.

"Robert Thornton, Murphy High News," Robert said solemnly. "Back to you, Sarah."

Sarah shook her head and laughed. "You're crazy, Robert!"

Sarah's cousin, Tasha Gordon, arrived moments later with Billy Simpson. Like Sarah, Tasha was a junior. She had come to Madison the year before to live with Sarah's family. Tasha's outgoing personality and talent on the girls' basketball team had soon made her popular at Murphy High. Dating Billy Simpson, the captain of the football team, didn't hurt, either. Today, Tasha was wearing faded jeans and a magenta T-shirt with a picture of Michael Jordan on it. Her pretty face was partially hidden under the baseball cap she wore, but there was no way to hide the long black hair that fell to her shoulders, or the smooth brown skin.

"Ugh," said Tasha when she glanced at Sarah's tray of food. The cafeteria was serving dry-looking squares of pizza, over-boiled carrots and peas, and a square of Jell-O that simply refused to jiggle.

"It's better than it looks," said Sarah.

"It *has* to be," said Tasha. Before she could sit down, she spied a white student heading toward a trash bin with his empty soda can. "Where are you going with that Coke can?" she called out.

When the startled boy turned around, Tasha pointed to a large cardboard box next to the door that led to the courtyard. "In there, please," she said. The boy obeyed.

"Your cousin is serious about recycling, isn't she?" Julie O'Connor whispered to Sarah as she placed her tray next to Cindy's and sat down.

"You got it," Sarah whispered back.

Cindy grinned. "Or maybe she just likes to boss people around."

"You know she's serious," said Sarah. "She got me to join the Ecology Club this semester, and she was the first person to sign up to empty the box when it gets full of cans."

"We need something better than a cardboard box," Tasha said, overhearing them. "The school should have permanent containers, like the ones they have up at Madison Community College—"

Before she could continue, Kevin Pardee approached

4

their table, tossing a basketball in his hands. "We're getting a game going outside," he told Dave and Billy. "Are you guys interested?"

"Let's go," said Dave, unfolding his long legs from under the table. He turned to Sarah. "You wanna watch?"

Sarah hesitated. She had planned to work on her English assignment, but the fresh spring air that blew into the cafeteria every time someone opened the door was irresistible. Everyone at the table got up to leave at once.

They made their way to the end of the faculty parking lot, where a few old basketball hoops dangled from poles. The teachers wisely parked far away from the hoops, since they were a favorite place for students to go when the weather turned warm.

From the soccer field, Steve Adams and April Winter waved to their friends. Steve had a Frisbee that was just a shade lighter than his own red hair. When he threw the Frisbee, Kwame and Cindy raced each other to get it. Sarah was tempted to join them, but she hung back to watch Dave play for a little while.

Julie O'Connor stayed with Sarah. "If we're lucky," she told her friend with a grin, "they'll get warm and take off their shirts."

The game began in earnest, and Dave dominated the makeshift court, whether he was playing defense or offense. Sarah stole a glance at Tasha, who stood watching the boys with unconcealed envy.

"If I had Dave's height and speed," Tasha murmured.

A few minutes later, Kevin Pardee let out a yell and clutched his ankle, grimacing with pain. The ball he had just stolen from Billy rolled toward Tasha. "I'm out," Kevin said, limping toward the school building.

Tasha retrieved the ball, planted her feet, and took a shot. The ball sailed through the basket.

"You want to play for him?" Dave asked her.

"Yeah, but I can't," said Tasha, pointing to the black leather shoes she wore.

"Here, Tasha," said Sarah, pulling off her own sneakers and giving them to her cousin. "Go get 'em."

Tasha was tying on the shoes when Marc Halle ran up and traded high fives with the other boys. "I'm in for Kevin," he announced.

"Hey, I'm in," said Tasha. "You can rotate in after me."

"Is she serious?" Marc Halle asked the other boys.

"You wait your turn like I did," said Tasha, not backing down.

"One of you get in here," said Dave, bouncing the ball impatiently.

"First one to miss from the foul line stays out, okay?" said Marc. Tasha hesitated. She was much better at layups, but she agreed.

She bounced the ball carefully, set her feet, and shot. The ball circled the rim twice before falling in. Sarah and Julie cheered.

Marc made his shot cleanly, and Tasha made hers again, this time bouncing it off the backboard. "It ain't pretty, but it works," she announced. But she had spoken too soon. She missed her next shot and walked back to the sidelines, disgusted.

"I'm not used to your shoes," she told Sarah.

"It doesn't matter," said Julie, glancing at her watch, "the bell is about to ring, anyway."

Thirty seconds later, it did.

"You got lucky on those free throws," Tasha told Marc Halle as they headed back to the cafeteria.

Marc grinned. "Maybe we should settle it with a little one-on-one," he said.

"Anytime," Tasha replied.

They joined the throng of students trying to squeeze through the cafeteria doors. Rick Hathaway, a tall blond junior, approached Marc.

"Hey, Marc, I got a joke for you," Rick said. "How do we know Santa Claus was a black man?"

Sarah stiffened, and Tasha turned toward Rick with a startled look on her face.

"I give up," Marc replied.

"Because only a black man would wear a red suit!"

"Ow," said Marc, making a face. "Man, that's lame."

Rick chuckled. "I heard it last night."

Tasha glared at him. "Hey, Rick. You like making racist jokes?"

"What are you talking about?" said Rick. Several students turned to look at them.

"Yo, it's just a dumb joke," said Marc, giving Tasha a playful pat on the arm. "I wasn't offended."

Tasha brushed aside Marc's hand. "Maybe you should have been."

"Lighten up, Tasha," said Rick with a nervous smile. He flipped the blond hair away from his face and hurried inside.

"What did Rick say?" said Kwame as they made their way into the building. "I was talking to Steve. I didn't hear it." Tasha repeated the joke, and Kwame frowned. "Let's go talk to him," he said.

Tasha led the way to Rick's table. Sarah went along, not sure why she hadn't been as offended as her cousin. To her, the joke was just dumb.

"Rick, do you know why I'm upset?" Tasha said, stepping in front of him to block his way.

"I don't know and I don't care," snapped Rick. "I wasn't talking to you, I was talking to Marc. He had no problem with what I said, and he's black."

"You're making a big deal over nothing," said Wayne Leatham, a white boy at Rick's table.

Tasha ignored him. "Rick, that joke was offensive to me as a black person."

"Free speech," muttered Wayne.

"Free speech, yes. But it was irresponsible," replied Kwame.

Rick rolled his eyes and exhaled loudly. "I don't believe this. You want an apology, Tasha? You got one. 'I'm sorry.' There. All better." He grabbed his books and led his friends past Tasha and the others.

"Not good enough," Tasha called after him. Her fists were clenched at her sides. When they were gone, she turned to find her friends giving her worried looks.

"What's the matter with you?" said Sarah as the

group walked toward their own book bags. "You're getting worked up over nothing. He didn't mean anything racist. It was just a dumb joke."

Kwame shook his head. "That's the sneakiest kind of racism," he said. "Jokes are easy to play down, but they remind people about false stereotypes, like the idea that all blacks are tacky dressers. That's just not true."

"No, Kwame, a joke is a joke," said Cindy firmly. "Back in Jamaica, my uncles tell jokes about Chinese people, American people, and anybody else they can think of. You're not supposed to take it seriously."

"I still think it was wrong," said Tasha. "And he's not going to get away with it." She walked off toward her class.

Sarah let out a loud sigh.

"Don't worry," said Cindy. "Tasha will get over it."

"Do *you* think Rick was racist?" Sarah asked her.

Cindy shook her head. "Maybe he used bad judgment, but that's all. Of course, if I'd heard a joke that dumb, I would have kept it to myself!"

Sarah laughed, but a part of her was still troubled. As she and Cindy were walking out of the cafeteria, Cindy pointed to a custodian out in the courtyard. He was making his way with a hose to the scrawled graffiti on the windowpanes. With a twist of the handle, he let the water splash across the letters, and "Murphy Rools" dissolved into foam.

After school, Sarah and Dave went to 18 Pine St., the pizza parlor where their friends liked to hang out.

A big group was already there when she and Dave arrived. Robert was telling Jennifer Wilson what Rick had said that afternoon. Steve Adams sat across from April and spoke to his girlfriend in hushed tones. Kwame was fanning his three pepperoni pizza slices, waiting for them to cool enough to eat. Billy was pointing at Cindy's open math book and explaining an equation to her.

"Where's Tasha?" Cindy asked Sarah.

"I thought she was here," said Sarah.

"Man, did you see her at lunch? She was buggin'!" said Dave.

Sarah nodded. Tasha's outburst in the cafeteria had been on her mind all afternoon. Is something wrong with me for not being more upset about Rick's joke? she wondered. Sometimes it seemed that way, especially when Tasha talked about Oakland, California, where she'd lived with her parents before they were killed in a car crash. Sarah had always lived in a middle-class suburban home. Her neighbors were mostly black people, but white people lived there, and so did many Asians. Growing up where she did, she didn't have to confront racism every day—even though she knew it was out there.

The sizzling sound of french fries cooking distracted her. She looked at Mr. Harris, the owner of the pizzeria, who had allowed her friends to place a framed collage of black heroes above their favorite booth in the back of his restaurant. At first, the picture had looked out of place next to the cowboy pictures hung up on the rest of

10

the wall, but now Sarah couldn't imagine sitting at the booth without seeing Martin Luther King, Frederick Douglass, Harriet Tubman, and the others. What would they do in a situation like this? she wondered.

"Yo, Tasha had a right to get mad," said Kwame through a mouthful of pizza.

Steve raked his red hair with his fingers. "Don't blacks tell jokes about white people? What about Richard Pryor and Eddie Murphy? They're no different."

"That's not the same thing. White folks have most of the money and political power in this country," Kwame pointed out. He held up three fingers. "I read somewhere that when blacks were slaves, the three things that kept their spirits alive were music, religion, and stories. Black folks *had* to make fun of their situation to ease the pain of racism. It is different."

Billy, who had been listening until now, looked at Kwame. "I know Rick Hathaway pretty well. He and Marc are tight because they live practically next door to each other. There's no way Rick is a racist."

"I didn't say he was," Kwame replied. "I said his joke was. And he was definitely insensitive to blacks for saying it."

"I agree with Kwame." Jennifer spoke up.

"I agree with Kwame, too," said April. Steve gave her a surprised look. "I know it's not the same thing, but some people like to tell dumb-blond jokes," she said, gesturing to her own hair. "Well, that's fine, but don't tell them in front of me. It makes me feel foolish, but if I get mad, they say I can't take a joke."

11

Dave raised his hand. "How many people here think the whole thing is being blown out of proportion?" Cindy, Steve, Billy, and Sarah raised their hands, but Robert, Jennifer, and Kwame kept theirs down. "Except for Steve, we're all black," Dave told Kwame. "You can't call *us* racially insensitive. I'm not saying I like what Rick did, but let's save our fights for the real problems. One joke by one person in one situation is not going to get me to sing 'We Shall Overcome'!"

Robert shook his head. "Man, this isn't about the joke. It's not about that at all." He looked at his friends and raised his hand. "How many people here think that Rick Hathaway owes Tasha an apology?" He smiled with satisfaction when Kwame, Jennifer, and April raised their hands.

"Count me in, too," said a familiar voice behind Kwame. He turned to find Tasha standing there.

"Where have you been?" Billy asked as she pulled a chair from a nearby table and joined the group.

"I had to take care of something in school," she said.

"She was probably writing graffiti on the lockers," Robert blurted. "Tasha is the Mad Soaper!" He turned Tasha's hands over. "See? her hands are clean!" Everyone laughed.

"No jokes about the Mad Soaper," said Billy, pretending to be serious. "I don't like anti-soap humor." Sarah, Cindy, and Dave laughed at that, but Tasha stiffened.

"I ain't done with Rick Hathaway," said Tasha. "He got off with a quick apology, but that just doesn't cut it.

12

He's going to have to apologize to me—to us," she said, pointing to her black friends. "And he's got to do it in public."

"How are you going to get him to do that?" said Steve.

"I'm going to make him apologize in the school paper," said Tasha. *The Murphy Monthly* never had a strict issue time. It came out sporadically, depending on how big the Journalism Club was that particular year. Lately, the paper managed to make it out twice a month.

"He'll never go for that," said Billy firmly.

"Hey, most white people didn't go for desegregation, but they had to do it," said Tasha.

"Can we talk about something else, please?" said Steve. His face flushed slightly when they turned to look at him. "I'm beginning to feel guilty, and I haven't done anything wrong. Be honest, folks," he said, raising his hand. "How many of the black people here have run into *real* racism?" He was shocked to see all his black friends raise their hands.

"Once, when my parents took me to Atlantic City for vacation, a group of kids on the beach called me Blackie the whole summer," said Billy.

"I was in a day camp and some white kids took my glasses when I was in the pool," Kwame recalled. "When I asked the boys to give me back my glasses, they said, 'Find them yourself, nigger.'"

Cindy nudged Sarah. "Remember that teacher in third grade, Mrs. Molitor? I don't think she ever called on any of us black kids the whole year we had her."

Sarah nodded.

"When I was in California visiting my aunt, I happened to be walking down the street with this white girl who lived next door. Suddenly, a car slowed down and a guy yelled at me to get away from her," Dave said.

"Well, shoot," said Billy with an exasperated laugh, "if we're going to start counting the times I've seen white women cross the street when they saw me coming..." He broke off.

An awkward silence fell over them. Steve shook his head and looked down at his plate. These were his friends. He couldn't believe they'd experienced hatred just because of the color of their skin.

Tasha finally spoke up. "So we're agreed. We're going to get Rick to apologize to us. We'll teach him and all the other white students a lesson."

"Let's not blow this out of proportion," Sarah replied slowly.

"Well, you're going to have to decide which side you're on, cuz," said Tasha, removing her cap and smoothing the hair underneath. "Because with or without you, I'm going to teach Rick Hathaway some manners!"

PINE

Two

The Gordon cousins didn't speak to each other on the way home from 18 Pine St. that afternoon. Dave had barely stopped his car before Tasha mumbled a quick thanks for the ride and hurried indoors.

"Excuse my cousin," said Sarah, giving Dave a peck on the cheek. "Thanks for the ride."

"No problem," said Dave. "Tasha'll cool down."

"I'm not even going to worry about it," said Sarah. She just wanted to finish her chores, get started on her homework, and put the whole Rick matter out of her mind.

When Sarah went into the basement to pick up a load of clothes from the dryer, she glanced at her father's workbench. A large tray of seedlings stood on it, and she smiled when she saw them. Every spring, Mr. Gordon vowed to make the garden better than ever. Sarah had not been surprised when he had come home a few weeks ago with the car's backseat full of seed packets, new garden tools, a drip hose, and two huge sacks of peat moss.

"Think of the money we'll save on vegetables," Mr. Gordon said every year.

Sarah went to the workbench to turn on the grow light above the seedlings. When the fluorescent light flickered on, she was shocked to find the plants looking withered and unhealthy. When she touched the growing mixture, it was hard and caked. She quickly filled a gardening can with water and gently moistened the soil in the tray.

She took the basket of clothes upstairs to her grandmother, Miss Essie. "Dad forgot to water his plants," she said.

"Your father has a lot on his mind these days, child," Miss Essie told her. "I'll give him a piece of *my* mind when he gets home."

"It's not like him," Sarah mused. She stayed in her grandmother's room after all the clothes had been folded and helped Miss Essie practice her lines for her latest play. Although she didn't travel much anymore, Miss Essie still performed in local theater, and had gone to New York recently to appear in a nationally broadcast coffee commercial. Looking at the posters and the press clippings framed on Miss Essie's wall made Sarah think about the all-black troupes that her grandmother had been a member of in the fifties and sixties.

"Miss Essie, would you say things are better for black

folks than they used to be?"

"Some things are," Miss Essie replied. "But we've all got a long way to go."

"You mean with white people?" Sarah asked.

"I mean 'folks' period," her grandmother replied. "Why do you ask?"

Sarah told her grandmother what Rick had said earlier that day. She was surprised to see Miss Essie frown at the feeble joke.

"Rick has to learn to choose his audience," Miss Essie sniffed. "How does Tasha know he was 'just kidding'?"

"Tasha called him a racist."

"Do _you_ think he is?"

Sarah tried to recall what she knew about Rick. He was in her history class, and he was one of the brighter students, always ready to argue a point with their teacher, Mrs. Parisi. When he gave an oral report, his voice carried a lot of enthusiasm. For some reason, Sarah always imagined him becoming a politician. "I don't think Rick is racist," she said finally. "But Tasha thinks he should apologize to her in public."

"So do I," Miss Essie replied, "but I wouldn't hold my breath." She handed Sarah a stack of towels and a pile of Mr. Gordon's socks. "From what you told me, Tasha confronted him in front of his friends, so it might hurt his pride to have to back down and apologize. He'd be losing face."

Sarah opened the hall closet next to the bathroom and placed the stack of folded towels on the shelf.

What Miss Essie had said about Rick's pride made sense. Rick might have been sorry he had offended Tasha, but he couldn't admit it in front of his friends. "He's not racist, just male!" Sarah would tell her cousin. She made her way to her parents' bedroom to put away the last of the laundry so that she could find Tasha and tell her.

When she opened the door, she had to stifle a shriek when a voice called out from the darkness of the room.

"Hi, Sarah."

"Mom! What are you doing here?" Sarah said, turning on the light. Her mother squinted at the sudden brightness. "Aren't you feeling well?"

"Just a little worn out," said Mrs. Gordon, sliding to a sitting position on the bed. Her face looked drawn and her hair was disheveled. In her job as a criminal lawyer, Mrs. Gordon often worked twelve-hour days at her office near city hall, and she would come home looking tired. But Sarah had never seen her like this.

"It has to be a pretty strong case of 'worn out' to keep you away from work," said Sarah. "Can I get you something?"

"No, I'm fine," said Mrs. Gordon. "What are you up to?"

Sarah placed the socks in her father's drawer and dragged the chair from the vanity to her mother's bedside. She was about to tell her mother about the joke incident when she noticed a few glossy pamphlets lying on the nightstand. Before she could pick one up, her mother took them away from the stand and moved them

18

to the other side of her bed.

"What are those?"

"Just some flyers I got from the doctor," said Mrs. Gordon, "nothing interesting."

"All right, what's wrong, Mom? You're not just feeling tired, are you?"

Mrs. Gordon sighed and glanced at the pamphlets. "Sarah, the truth is I don't know what's wrong. I went to the doctor a few days ago for some routine tests, and they found something surprising—"

"What do they think it might be?" asked Sarah. Her heart began beating loudly in her chest when Mrs. Gordon asked her to close the door. She was worried for her mother, and a little unnerved that she was carrying such a big secret.

"It's a woman's problem," Mrs. Gordon began. "A few days ago, I began to feel dizzy, and I was throwing up a lot. So I went to the doctor for some tests. I won't know for sure about anything until the results come back from the lab."

"Yes, but what did he test for?" Sarah pressed further.

"The doctor is a she," Mrs. Gordon corrected. "And she ran a variety of tests. If it's positive, we'll celebrate in style!"

"Mom, you're not telling anything! You say it's a woman's problem, but what kind? I know you're not pregnant."

Mrs. Gordon arched an eyebrow and tried to hide a smile. "How do *you* know I'm not pregnant? Do you think I'm too old to have another child? Getting pregnant in your forties is a bit uncommon, but it's not impossible."

"Do you have sickle-cell anemia or diabetes or something?"

Mrs. Gordon laughed. "Please, Sarah! Do I look like I'm that sick?" Her expression turned serious and she lowered her voice to a whisper. "Look, honey, your father and I don't want anyone in the family to know what this is about until the tests come back. Will you let us keep it from you for a few days?"

Before Sarah could answer, Mr. Gordon entered the bedroom. Sarah's father had a glass of orange juice in his hand, which he gave to Mrs. Gordon.

"Thanks for taking care of my tomato plants, Sarah," said Mr. Gordon, as he sat down on the bed. "Your grandmother just scolded me about leaving them to die."

"Dad, Mom won't tell me why she's in bed."

"It's our little secret," he said, giving his wife a kiss. "How do you feel?"

"Better," Mrs. Gordon replied.

"Any temperature? Do you want some food?"

"I'm fine, Donald." Mrs. Gordon gestured toward Sarah. "Your daughter thinks I'm too old to have another baby."

"Not quite yet," said Mr. Gordon.

By the way her father was talking to her mother, cooing and kissing her forehead, Sarah sensed it was time to leave. "I'd better look at that homework," she said, sliding the chair back under the vanity.

"Don't tell anyone about the doctor visit," her mother called after her as she left.

How can I tell them something I don't even know myself? Sarah wondered.

Mrs. Gordon didn't come down for dinner that evening. Mr. Gordon told Tasha and Sarah's twelve-year-old sister, Allison, that Mrs. Gordon was exhausted.

"She can't be too tired to have some of my famous stuffed peppers," Miss Essie declared. "I'll fix a plate and take it up to her."

Sarah noticed that her cousin was not her usual talkative self. Could she still be thinking about Rick? she wondered. Suddenly, she had an idea. "Dad," she said. "I heard a riddle today."

"Lay it on me," said Mr. Gordon.

"How do we know Santa Claus is black?" said Sarah. Mr. Gordon shrugged. "Because only a black man would wear a red suit."

Mr. Gordon let out a short laugh, and Sarah nudged Tasha with her foot. "See?" she whispered to her cousin.

"You're not a white boy," Tasha told her. "It's different if it's told just between us."

"I don't get it," said Allison. "Why would a black man own a red suit any more than a white man?"

Mr. Gordon explained the stereotype that blacks were tacky dressers to Allison, and Sarah no longer felt smug. Tasha told her uncle what had happened earlier that day, and the expression on her father's face made her feel even worse.

"I hope those jokes aren't part of a trend," said Mr. Gordon.

"But you laughed, Dad!" Sarah cried.

"Sometimes you can't control what makes you laugh," said Mr. Gordon. "I can see how some black students could get angry at that."

It was Tasha's turn to nudge Sarah's foot.

Miss Essie returned to the dining room with the untouched plate. "She said she wasn't hungry at all. I was going to leave it on her nightstand for later, but she said no."

"I hope it's not the flu," said Tasha.

Sarah remembered the pamphlets on the nightstand. Could they have been about the flu? she wondered. The conversation went back to Rick's joke. When Miss Essie brought up the possibility of a private apology from Rick to spare his pride, Tasha shook her head.

"I don't care about his wounded male pride. He insulted me in public, he should have to apologize in public," said Tasha. She gave Sarah a meaningful stare. "And I'm not going to let it go until he does."

"Whoa," said Mr. Gordon. "One crusade at a time." He pointed to Tasha and Sarah. "Which one of you Ecology Club members is going to the school board meeting with me tomorrow to ask for recycling bins?"

"I am," said Tasha. "But this race thing is more important than that."

Mr. Gordon shook his head. "Your responsibility to the Eco Club is just as important. When you come with me tomorrow, you're going to have to address the school board," he reminded her. "That means getting up in front of a microphone and convincing the school board they should buy the recycling bins."

"I know, Uncle Donald," said Tasha with a hint of impatience. "I've got a little speech all written out."

"The club also put together a list of students who pledged to recycle. Almost every Murphy kid signed the pledge," Sarah added.

"Terrific," said Mr. Gordon, pleased. "I'm proud that you girls are involved in this."

After dinner, Tasha followed Mr. Gordon into the den. "You didn't forget your promise, did you, Uncle Donald?"

"Of course not," said Mr. Gordon as he turned on the television to the evening news. "What did I promise?"

"You were going to take me driving this week," Tasha reminded him.

"Let's see: Today is Tuesday, so I've got five days to make good," said Mr. Gordon, giving his niece a tired smile. "We'll drive around after the school board meeting tomorrow."

"You promised last week it would be today," said Tasha.

Mr. Gordon sighed. He turned his attention to the news. "I said tomorrow, and I mean it, Tasha."

Tasha stormed into Sarah's room. "Your father is impossible," she declared. "He promised to drive me around the Hamilton High parking lot tonight."

"He's got other things on his mind," said Sarah, thinking of her mother's spending the whole day in bed.

"Then it's time to go to Plan B," said Tasha.

Sarah followed her cousin to the hallway and watched as Tasha dialed Billy Simpson's number.

"Hi, Billy. Can you pick me up tonight? I want to do that thing we talked about." She hung up a few moments later. Tasha cast a wary look at Miss Essie's room before adding in a whisper, "If Uncle Donald won't teach me to drive, Billy will."

"You know he can't do that!" cried Sarah. "One of the drivers has to be over twenty-one; it says so in the learner's permit booklet." She gave her cousin an accusing look. "Something tells me this isn't the first time you two have done this."

"Well, what if it isn't?" Tasha replied.

Sarah followed Tasha into her bedroom, where she watched her cousin select a blue suede jacket from her closet. "It's dangerous, cuz."

"Billy and I are very careful. We only go to the Westcove Mall and drive around the parking lot. You can practice everything there: parallel parking, left turns, k-turns—"

"And fender benders!" Sarah finished for her. "Why don't you wait until Dad takes you?"

"He's always busy," said Tasha, putting on her jacket and placing her learner's permit in a small purse. "I don't want to wait until summer vacation to take my driving test. I want that license before I turn seventeen!"

"But driving around with Billy? Don't you remember what happened to me last year?"

Tasha had no trouble recalling the accident Jennifer Wilson had had with her mother's car. Sarah had been in that car as well, and the collision had left her in a coma for a week. "That's totally different," Tasha replied. "Besides, I'm not going to let your accident stop me from learning how to drive. Or any other accident, for that matter," she muttered.

For a second, Sarah didn't know what "other accident" Tasha was talking about. Then she remembered the accident that had killed Tasha's parents. "I don't know why you tell me these things," Sarah snapped. "If you want to go driving with Billy, that's your business, but don't tell me about it!"

"Fine," said Tasha. She suddenly grinned. "You worry too much, cuz."

"And you don't worry enough!" Sarah shot back.

"You're right, of course," said Cindy later that evening when Sarah called her. "Tasha's going to do what Tasha's going to do, but she shouldn't get you involved."

Julie O'Connor was listening from another phone at Cindy's house. "You're not going to tell your parents, are you?"

"Of course not," Sarah answered. "I don't tattle." Sarah looked up from the phone in the hallway and lowered her voice in case Allison or Miss Essie was nearby. "And I think Billy's a good driver, but Tasha can be so . . . temperamental! I wonder how she handles herself behind a wheel."

"I bet she's good," said Julie. "My dad is a lot like Tasha, and when he's behind the wheel, we *fly*! But my mom takes her time, she's very careful. But here's the thing: she's crumpled two fenders in the last year, and my dad hasn't ever been in an accident."

"That doesn't prove anything," said Cindy firmly. "Your mother may have just been unlucky."

"It comes down to confidence," said Julie matter-of-factly. "My mom admits it. Sometimes she gets hyper behind the wheel."

Sarah listened with mounting worry. She suspected she would be a cautious, scared driver rather than a bold, confident one when her turn came. She was suddenly tired of thinking about driving and accidents. "Hey, Cindy, how old was April's stepmother when she got pregnant?"

"Pretty old," said Cindy. "In her late thirties."

"Late thirties, early forties?" Sarah pressed. When Julie asked why she wanted to know, Sarah told them about the conversation she had had earlier that afternoon with her mother. "She won't tell me what the problem is, but she said it was a woman's problem. And when Dad walked in to see her, he was acting all lovey-dovey."

"It could be!" Cindy declared.

"I'm not saying it's true," Sarah said hastily. "It could be something else. Something worse."

"Is she tired? Is she finicky about what she eats?"

asked Julie. When Sarah said yes, Julie let out a gleeful laugh. "Start knitting them booties, girl."

Sarah began to wonder if it had been a good idea to tell them. "Look," she said quickly, "don't tell anyone about this, okay? Tasha doesn't even know, and Mom didn't tell me she was pregnant. She gets some tests back later this week."

"In that case, it must be something else," said Julie. "They have all sorts of home pregnancy tests you can buy in the drugstore. If she were pregnant, she could have bought one and known the same day."

"Maybe she did, and then went to the doctor to make sure," Cindy told her friend.

Sarah thought about that possibility. She thought again about the chance that it might be something dire, but her mother had not looked *that* sick—just drawn, and perhaps a little thinner than usual. Sarah sat on the floor of the hallway, listening to her friends go on about old people they knew who had had children. But her mind began to wander, and she remembered the plants in the basement Mr. Gordon had neglected. Whatever her mother had, it had to be important for her father to forget his seedlings. She said good-bye to Cindy and Julie and returned to her room.

Five minutes later, the phone rang again.

"Cameron!" April shouted, just as Sarah was saying hello.

"April, what are you talking about?"

"Call him Cameron if it's a boy, and Crystal if it's a girl," said April. "I just got off the phone with Cindy, and she told me the news. Congratulations, Sarah!"

"Wait a minute!" Sarah began. But getting April to stop talking was harder than getting her to start. Sarah stifled a helpless laugh as she sat down and listened to the ordeals April had gone through when her step-mother was pregnant with Justin.

"He's so beautiful!" April cried. "What about you? Would you want a little brother or a little sister?"

"A little brother," said Sarah, letting herself be swept up in April's enthusiasm. "I've already got a little sister, and with Tasha and Miss Essie, poor Dad is really out-numbered."

When Sarah hung up and returned to her homework, she was feeling better. She glanced at her room: it was messier than she ordinarily kept it. The nice days had made her turn out her dresser, looking for shorts and T-shirts that had been hidden since September. On top of her dresser, she saw the framed pictures of her family. Tasha's photograph had been the latest addition. Would there soon be one more? she wondered.

18 PINE

Three

"Eyes front, Tasha," Mr. Cala warned.

It was Wednesday morning, and Tasha sat in her math class trying to focus on the homework she had done last night after her driving lesson with Billy. She watched as Mr. Cala wrote a series of problems on the blackboard, then drew a perfect chalk circle with one sweep of his arm. Even after she'd seen it all year, it remained an impressive trick.

She gave Mr. Cala her full attention for the next few minutes, but couldn't sit still for very long. She was a little nervous about the recycling speech she would have to give at the school board meeting that evening. Also, Connie, who sat next to her, had asked her for details of her argument with Rick the day before.

Tasha kept an eye on Mr. Cala. "He made a racist

joke, and now he won't apologize for it," she whispered to Connie.

"What was the joke?" said Connie.

"What's the difference?" Tasha said impatiently. Everyone had asked her the same question. Even though most of her friends were upset about the situation, they wanted to hear the joke for themselves. Some of her friends had even laughed, until they saw Tasha's stern face. She whispered the joke again, and watched Connie shake her head.

"Tasha, is there something wrong with your chair? You seem to be leaning to the left," Mr. Cala commented dryly. The class giggled.

Tasha felt her face getting warm. "I'm fine."

"Good," said Mr. Cala. "This material is hard enough without having to pause every two minutes to get your attention."

"I'm sorry, Mr. Cala. I have a lot on my mind," said Tasha truthfully.

"Well, make some room in there for math, please," said Mr. Cala.

The next time Tasha was caught talking, Mr. Cala didn't bother to ask her what the problem was. Instead, he pointed to the door and waited for Tasha to close her books, pick up her things, and leave the room.

"I'll tell Mr. Schlesinger you're on your way," Mr. Cala said grimly. He closed the door to his classroom and stood out in the hallway with her. "This isn't like you, Tasha. If something is bothering you, talk to me about it after class, or to a counselor. But I have twenty other students who aren't as good at this stuff as you are. Do you understand?"

Tasha nodded. She walked slowly down the hall, in no particular hurry to face the vice principal. Mr. Schlesinger's temper was legendary among the high school students. Even the junior high students knew about him well before they came to Murphy.

"You're one of Murphy High's brightest students," Mr. Schlesinger began when Tasha sat on the battered couch in his office. It was all Tasha could do to restrain herself from saying the words along with him. Everyone who reported to Mr. Schlesinger "was one of Murphy High's brightest students."

"Yes, Mr. Schlesinger," she said humbly.

"Then why can't you concentrate in class?" he said, slapping his hand two times on the metal desktop. It sounded like a drum. He turned to the window and sighed loudly. "I don't need any more work than I already have. So please stay out of trouble, so I can concentrate on the bad apples in the school."

Tasha gave him a convincing look of sorrow as Mr. Schlesinger spoke on about responsibility and education. Suddenly he turned to face her. "You wouldn't happen to know who's been soaping the walls, would you?"

The question came from out of the blue, and Tasha was taken aback. "I have no idea, sir," she said truthfully.

"No one does," muttered Mr. Schlesinger. He told Tasha to wait out the rest of the period in the conference room next to his office.

* * *

"It was Rick's fault I got in trouble," Tasha told Jennifer at lunch that afternoon.

Jennifer shook her head and glared at Rick Hathaway. On the other side of the room, he and a friend were batting an empty milk carton across a table.

"The reason you got busted was because you were talking," Sarah pointed out. "Mr. Cala still would have gotten mad, no matter what you were talking about."

"I was talking to Jennifer," Tasha said, giving her cousin a frosty look.

"Excuse *me*," said Sarah. Her anger turned to worry as she scanned her table of friends. The argument at 18 Pine St. the day before had left an uneasy feeling among the group. Steve usually chatted with Kwame and April, but today he sat with Billy. Robert, who usually traded friendly insults with Billy, was doing his best to ignore him. Sarah brightened when she saw Dave approaching.

"Hey, Sarah, what's going on with your mom?"

"Why do you ask?" said Sarah. "Did Cindy call you and tell you she was pregnant?"

Dave looked confused. "No. My mom said she saw her leaving the hospital the day before yesterday." He gave her a sheepish grin. "Mom has me on a fact-finding mission."

Sarah remembered that Mrs. Hunter did volunteer work at the hospital. "I don't know anything except that she's been feeling run-down," said Sarah, raising her hand. "Word of honor, that's it."

32

"That's not going to satisfy my mom, but I did my best," said Dave. He shook his head. "She's so nosy! She's got to know everything that's going on in the neighborhood."

"I'm going to call Mom this afternoon and get to the bottom of this. Whatever it is, I have a right to know," said Sarah.

Mr. Rowland approached their table. He was the faculty adviser for the Ecology Club. "There you are," he said when he spied Tasha. "I hope you didn't forget your tour of the kitchen." At the last meeting, Tasha had suggested they look for ways to prevent food waste by inspecting the cafeteria.

"No, sir," said Tasha, standing up.

"Any time you're ready. I'll tell them you're on your way."

As soon as Mr. Rowland was out of earshot, Tasha turned to her cousin.

"Listen," she said urgently. "Can you go for me, Sarah?"

"Wait a minute, girl. It's your speech tonight, remember?" Sarah picked up Tasha's notebook and held it out to her. Tasha reluctantly took it. "What's the matter with you, Tasha?" Sarah asked as they headed for the kitchen. "This recycling drive was all you talked about for weeks, and suddenly one joke makes you forget everything."

"How can I worry about a few soda cans when we have this prejudiced white boy thinking he can say anything he wants?" said Tasha. She turned and pointed to their table. "Do you remember when Steve asked us if we had ever come across racism? Do you remember the look on his face when we told him we had?"

Sarah nodded.

"He couldn't believe it!" said Tasha. "And that got me thinking: If Steve doesn't know what we blacks go through, what about other white kids? I want to get Rick to understand what we put up with. That's what I want to work on—not this," she said, gesturing at the cafeteria.

"How are you going to do that?" Sarah asked. She pushed against the swinging doors, and they entered the noisy kitchen.

"You'll see," said Tasha.

Once they were in the kitchen, Mr. Rowland left them with a tall white woman who introduced herself as Joanne.

"If you have any questions, just let me know," said Joanne.

The Gordon cousins observed the busy women. One stood over a serving table, scraping the last servings of vegetables into a metal canister before covering the top with plastic and putting it into the freezer.

"Are they going to use those vegetables tomorrow?"

"Sure," said Joanne, "but not the way you saw them. They'll probably be used in vegetable soup." She smiled. "See? We recycle, too."

The Gordon cousins were taken to the back lot where the freezer trucks brought the prepared dishes such as lasagna squares and chicken wings to the school. "We don't have time to make those ourselves. All we do is reheat them here," said Joanne. "Any questions so far?"

Tasha, who was supposed to be asking questions, looked slightly bored. Sarah felt embarrassed by the silence. "We're supposed to find ways for the kitchen to cut waste," said Sarah. "Do you have any ideas?"

Joanne shook her head. "We do the best we can with what we've got back here. But we don't waste; the students do. Come on, I'll show you." She guided them to a room where Sarah could hear a loud humming. When Joanne opened the door, she shouted a greeting to a large black woman named Irene.

Irene wore a net over her copper-colored hair. Her top lip was pleated with wrinkles, and a slight mustache was visible. She was perched on a high stool in front of a conveyor belt, which brought the used lunch trays to her. She dumped the food scraps into a trough with running water, which carried the waste to a large compactor.

Many of the trays had untouched food on them. Joanne pointed to them. "See what I mean?" she said. "It's the students who waste."

"Maybe they'd eat more of it if the food wasn't so..." Sarah stopped before she said something that might hurt Joanne's feelings. "Uh. Sometimes the food is a little bland."

"We can't get too fancy," said Joanne. "The food has to appeal to everyone, so it can't be too spicy or exotic or anything." She excused herself and left the Gordon consins with Irene.

"I don't usually do this by myself," Irene explained, "but my coworker is sick today." She pressed a button underneath the counter and stopped the food disposal machine's blade.

"What happens to the food once it goes through here?" Sarah asked, pointing to the compactor.

"I don't know," said the woman. "Into the sewer, I guess."

"Doesn't the smell get to you after a while?" Tasha asked.

Brilliant recycling question! Sarah thought.

"Honey, everything gets to me after a while," said Irene with a short laugh. "But what are you going to do? You can get used to anything." She pointed to the compactor. "I don't know if this would help your recycling project, but I always thought it was a shame to send all that chopped-up food to the sewer. I would sell the waste to a farmer so he could use it for compost. It's just food and some Popsicle sticks in there."

"Sounds like you've given this a lot of thought," said Tasha.

"This job gives you a lot of time to do that," said Irene with a laugh that ended in a sigh. "It's nice to see young girls like you interested in these things. Are you two going to college?"

"Definitely," they both said.

"Good," Irene said. "I always wish I had. But I grew up in a small town in the South. If you weren't the minister's kid, or the doctor's kid, you were out of luck as far as college went."

For the first time, Tasha appeared interested. They thanked Irene and left. The air in the dishwashing room had been hot and damp. Once they left, the dryer air felt cool against their faces.

"Did you notice they put the black woman in that hot room?" said Tasha. "They work her like a dog!"

"Whoa, Tasha," said Sarah. "This is a kitchen. Did you expect to see people holding pencils and making phone calls?"

Before leaving, Sarah found Joanne and thanked her for the visit.

"My pleasure," said Joanne. "Any last questions?"

"Yes," said Tasha, speaking to her for the first time. "Why is Ms. Irene stuck in that hot dishwashing room while the white ladies are on the serving line?"

Joanne's eyebrows shot up, and Sarah stifled an overwhelming urge to slap her cousin.

"Come with me," said Joanne coldly. She took the Gordons to a chart on the back wall and pointed to Irene's name. "She's only in there for two weeks, then she's back on the serving line or preparing food. We all rotate the jobs. That answer your question?"

"Thank you," said Tasha.

The dismissal bell rang just then, and Sarah almost ran out of the kitchen.

"I've never been so embarrassed in my life!" Sarah cried, striding back to their table.

"I had to know!"

"I was thinking you might be right about Rick and everything, but you went too far back there," said Sarah hotly. "You're seeing racism where there isn't any!"

Tasha didn't answer. She spied Rick Hathaway crossing the courtyard alone and ran toward him. "Rick, wait up. I have to talk to you."

Rick stopped when he saw the Gordon cousins approaching. He had a tense, distracted look on his face, and he glowered at them. "If you think I'm going to apologize to you, Tasha, you're wrong." He thrust a finger at Tasha's face. "*You're* the one who should be apologizing to me. You embarrassed me in front of half the school yesterday, and I'm getting a lot of heat for it."

"Maybe it will make you think twice about what you say," said Tasha.

"I don't have to think twice, because I haven't done anything wrong," he snapped. "Now half the school thinks I'm prejudiced, but I'm not. I hate racism! Marc Halle is one of my best friends. But in this country, we have the right to say whatever we want—"

Tasha interrupted. "But if what you say turns out to hurt someone—"

Rick waved his hand impatiently. "My stupid joke didn't hurt anyone! I know you, Tasha. You like to be the center of attention, and this is just a way for you to get some. Stop playing yourself off as a victim!" He stormed away.

"See, Sarah?" said Tasha. "He refuses to admit anything. And this time his friends weren't around, so he didn't have to lose face. He could have said, 'I'm sorry.'"

"Did you say 'I'm sorry' when you practically accused Joanne of racism in the kitchen?"

Tasha turned to face her cousin. "What is the matter with you? I'm the one you should be defending—your cousin. Your *black* cousin. Not some white dude who doesn't know how to show your people respect."

"Just a minute," Sarah began. She could feel her face getting warm.

"You worry too much about the wrong people," said Tasha. With that, she headed back into the building.

"Come back here and finish what you started!" Sarah called after her. She wanted to go after Tasha, but her art class was in the opposite direction. She barely made it into the class before the tardy bell rang, and she brooded for the entire period.

"You look like you're having a bad day," said Cindy when Sarah appeared at her locker at the end of the afternoon.

"Between Tasha giving me grief for not being black enough, and my mother keeping secrets about her health from me, I'm not having a good one," Sarah admitted.

"Are you going to sign the petition?" said Cindy.

Sarah was surprised by the question. The Ecology Club had circulated a petition to find out how many students would support recycling. "I was the one who got you to sign, remember? Tasha's going to turn it in to the school board tonight."

"Not the recycling petition, this one," said Cindy. She produced a sheet of legal-sized copy paper from her locker and handed it to Sarah. "Kwame's idea. He printed it out in computer class and started passing it around."

Sarah read the petition.

Resolved: We, the students of Murphy High, reject racism in speech or action, and any other prejudice against people because of their color, religion, gender, or ethnic origin. We demand that any examples of prejudice be met with suspension or expulsion.

Kwame's signature appeared below, followed by Tasha's, then Jennifer Wilson's, José Melendez's, Robert Thornton's, and finally Cindy Phillips's.

Sarah glanced at her friend. "I thought you agreed that Rick's joke was just a joke."

Cindy looked uncomfortable. "Sure, but this petition doesn't talk about that. All it says is that I'm against racism. We all are."

"What does Kwame want to do with this petition? Is he going to turn it in to someone?"

Cindy shrugged. "I don't know. I think he's just trying to make a statement."

Sarah looked at the petition again. There was nothing she objected to. As she was signing her name to it, a wonderful idea suddenly came to her. "Cindy, we can put an end to this whole mess in a minute!" she said excitedly. She giggled at Cindy's confused look. "All we've got to do is get Rick to sign this."

The thought of presenting Kwame with the petition signed by Rick made her smile. She had been there when Rick said he hated racism. Shoot, Tasha might even take it as a kind of apology, Sarah thought. "Can I keep this for a while?" Sarah asked her friend.

She found Rick sitting on the low wall that circled the flagpole, waiting for his bus. He wore a Walkman, and his head bobbed silently to the music. He didn't hear Sarah approaching, and was a little startled when she handed him the petition.

Rick scowled as he scanned what Kwame had written.

"It doesn't say anything about you," Sarah pointed out. "It just says you're against racism."

"I am," said Rick shaking his head slowly, "but I can't sign this."

"Why not?" said Sarah. "It'll get people off your back."

"I agree with everything in the petition," Rick declared. "Except this part that says *racism in speech or action*. Who's going to decide what's racist speech or action? Tasha?" He laughed hollowly.

"Words can hurt, Rick," said Sarah. "If you yell 'fire' in a crowded theater and someone gets hurt running for the door, you're responsible for that."

"I totally agree. But saying Santa Claus must be black because he has a red suit isn't the same as yelling fire in a theater." Rick gave Sarah a troubled look. "I'm getting a lot of flak over what I said, but apologizing to Tasha won't change how I feel about it inside. It would be dishonest." He waved the petition. "I guess this means she hasn't forgotten about it."

"She hasn't. And I wouldn't wait for her to get over it,

41

either. Tasha's pretty stubborn," said Sarah.

As he handed back the petition, Rick gave Sarah a determined look. "So am I," he said.

Disgusted, Sarah folded the petition carefully and put it in her backpack.

Instead of meeting her friends at 18 Pine St. that afternoon, Sarah went to the pay phones near the main office and called her house to check on her mother.

"Your mother went to work today," Miss Essie told her. "She got up after you kids left for school. I told her to stay home, but she said she was feeling better and took off."

"Time to get to the bottom of this," Sarah said as she hung up.

She took a city bus downtown to Madison City Hall, walked half a block to her mother's office building, and ran up the steps, scattering the pigeons that waddled about.

Sarah found her mother in the firm's reference library, murmuring notes into a pocket tape recorder. "Hey, Ma," said Sarah cheerfully. "Feeling better?"

"Yes, thank you," said Mrs. Gordon. She removed her reading glasses and looked at her daughter. "What brings you here, Sarah?"

Sarah took the seat next to her mother, planted her elbows on the table, and stared levelly at her. "Please tell me what's wrong with you."

Mrs. Gordon smiled. "If I said it was the flu, would you be satisfied?"

Sarah shook her head.

Mrs. Gordon sighed. "I didn't think so." She leaned across the table and spoke softly. "As you know, I've been feeling under the weather lately. I didn't know what was wrong with me, so I went to the doctor the day before yesterday. She gave me a complete checkup, and she found a lump in my left breast."

"Oh no!"

"The doctor performed a biopsy. That means she took a tissue sample from the growth and sent it to a lab to be analyzed." She looked at her daughter. "I didn't want anyone to know about it until I got the report back, because it could be nothing."

"Those pamphlets and papers you had on the bed: Were they about cancer?" said Sarah after a long silence.

"Breast cancer, yes. I was preparing myself for the worst," her mother replied. "But that's only the worst-case scenario," she added hastily. "The tumor could be benign."

"Tumor!"

"That's what they found," said Mrs. Gordon. "Don't let the name scare you. It's just some tissue that kept on growing when it should have stopped. Most tumors are just fatty cells and water." She glanced around the law library. "I never thought I'd be telling you here, but last night I decided you should know. If it turns out to be cancer, then I don't want it to come as a surprise to you."

Sarah blinked. Cancer? Her mother? Even a benign

tumor sounded ominous. She stared at her mother with tear-filled eyes.

"Baby, you look so scared!" Mrs. Gordon said softly. "Maybe I shouldn't have told you. I kept going back and forth, wondering whether to—"

"No." Sarah shook her head. "I wanted to know."

"For now, only your father and you know about the biopsy," Mrs. Gordon told her. "I haven't even told Miss Essie. No use getting everyone upset until we learn the truth about this. That's why I want you to be brave, and not tell Tasha or Allison. We'll keep this between the three of us until we have more information."

"When did you start thinking there was something wrong? How big is the lump? Does it hurt? Why aren't you in the hospital?" The questions formed and reformed in Sarah's mind, and Mrs. Gordon patiently answered them. The lump didn't hurt. She felt fine, just a little under the weather. She wouldn't go to the hospital until the report came back.

"Whether the report is good news or bad news, I'm going to get that lump removed," Mrs. Gordon told her. Then she glanced at her watch and gave her daughter an apologetic look. "I'm sorry, baby, but I have a meeting with a client in a half hour, and I have to look over this material."

Sarah stood up to go.

"Your father insisted that I stay home yesterday, but I got very scared just lying on the bed. I think the best thing for me is to keep on working until we know for sure."

"When will that be?" Sarah asked.

"Could be as soon as tomorrow," said Mrs. Gordon. She accompanied Sarah to the building lobby, then gave her daughter a hug. "We'll get through it," she said.

Outside, Sarah took in a few gulps of air. She walked to the bus stop without once looking up from the sidewalk. She found herself thinking about the woman in the dishwashing room at school. "You can get used to anything," Irene had said. Sarah wondered if she could get used to her mother's having cancer, or possibly dying.

It didn't take long before the bus arrived. It was already crowded with people going home from work, and she didn't find a seat until she was more than halfway home. When she sat down, Sarah turned to look out the window so that no one would see her cry.

Four

Sarah spent the rest of the afternoon writing in her diary about her mother's breast tumor, and crying when she ran out of words to write. She had little appetite at dinner, and Mr. Gordon kept asking if she was all right. She was sitting at her desk, staring blankly at her chemistry homework, when Tasha came in and announced she was not going to the school board meeting.

"What do you mean you're not going to the meeting!"

"You don't have to shout," said Tasha. "I can always give the speech next Wednesday."

"I'm afraid not," said Mr. Gordon. He stood in Sarah's doorway, handsome in his gray suit. "The next open meeting is a month away."

"See?" said Sarah. "You'll be letting everybody down."

47

"I can't go, Uncle Donald," said Tasha firmly. "I promised Kwame I'd help him tonight. We're going to call as many black Murphy High students as we can, and get them to wear kente cloth tomorrow to show black pride." She held up a cap made of the colorful African weave.

"You knew you had this meeting tonight," said Mr. Gordon.

"I'm sorry," said Tasha. "I think this is more important."

"Then I guess our driving lesson is off, too," said Mr. Gordon. "When you can show me you can live up to your responsibilities, we can resume the lessons."

Sarah got up and snatched her jacket from the coat hook behind the door. "Just a minute, Dad," she called out. "*I'm* going." She turned back to Tasha. "The Ecology Club was counting on you!"

"And I would have gone, too, if Rick hadn't proved there was racism in the school," Tasha countered. She went to her room and returned with her backpack. She pulled out the clipboard that held her speech and the petitions. "See? The speech is finished. Your dad probably thinks I wasn't prepared," Tasha said with a slight trembling in her voice. "It wasn't that."

The last thing in the world Sarah wanted to do was to stand before a group of grown-ups to read a speech. But Tasha had promised the Ecology Club a report at their meeting on Friday. As mad as she was at Tasha, she didn't want the club members to be angry with her cousin. She even found herself defending Tasha when Mr. Gordon complained about her last-minute change of plans.

"She really believes Rick's joke was harmful," said Sarah.

"You know," said Mr. Gordon, "sometimes jokes have a grain of truth to them. When I was in college, my roommate showed up for a date in a yellow suit."

"So you think Tasha is overdoing it?"

Mr. Gordon watched the traffic in front of him. "Well, I'm not really sure," he said after a while. "If I felt there was meanness behind the joke, then I'd probably feel like Tasha does."

Sarah had wanted to tell her father that she knew about her mother's lump and the biopsy, but Mr. Gordon began to talk about other college memories, and Sarah didn't want to ruin his cheerful mood.

When they arrived at the Board of Education building, Sarah felt a little let down. She had expected to see a crowded hall with high ceilings, almost like a church, where important issues were debated. Instead, she found herself in an oversized conference room with folding chairs to sit on, and only a row of tables separating the members of the school board from everyone else. She was more surprised to see only ten or twelve people attending the meeting.

"This is a pretty good turnout," Mr. Gordon whispered before taking his seat behind the conference table.

While the school board took up other matters, Sarah

went over the statement Tasha had written, adding a few points of her own and removing some of the phrases she didn't feel comfortable saying.

When the time came to hear the motions and petitions, Sarah's pulse began to quicken. A woman stood up and complained for what felt like an hour about her son's morning walk to his bus stop. "It's two blocks away," she said angrily. "It's too long for him to walk, especially in the winter. He's got short legs!" She demanded that the board provide a stop closer to her home. The school board promised to look into the matter.

Finally, it was Sarah's turn.

"Mr. Superintendent," she said, mimicking the way the previous speakers had addressed the board, "I represent the members of the Murphy High School Ecology Club. We would like the school board to consider putting more recycling bins in the cafeteria and in the activities room where they sell snacks." She read the rest of the paper, including the suggestion that they consider using the cafeteria waste food as fertilizer. This brought a smile from some members of the school board.

"That sounds like a reasonable request," said a woman on the board who smiled at Sarah. Sarah smiled back, but her optimism faded when she heard a familiar voice from the back of the room. She turned around and saw Mr. Schlesinger standing near the door.

"I'm afraid that the recycling idea is a little ahead of its time for Murphy High," said Mr. Schlesinger. "The fact is, our part of town has only one waste pickup per week. Paper, plastic, and other items would create a sanitation problem. I won't even touch the problems involved with transporting food waste. Furthermore, there are eight hundred students at Murphy High. If we started recycling, those bins would have to be emptied every day. That means hiring more custodians, or paying overtime to the ones we already have."

Sarah felt her face warming up as she leaned into the microphone to answer Mr. Schlesinger's arguments. It felt odd to be arguing with the vice principal of her school in front of her father. "Mr. Superintendent, if the problem is the weekly pickup, can't the school set aside some money for the truck to come twice a week?"

"We can't afford it right now," said Mr. Parrish. "But thank you. We will certainly keep your Economy Club suggestions in mind."

It's Ecology, not Economy, thought Sarah. Dejected, she moved away from the microphone. She glanced at her father, who was frowning at Mr. Parrish. Before sitting down, Sarah placed the stack of petitions on the table in front of the woman who was taking the minutes of the meeting. "Almost half the students are willing to use the recycling bins if they're brought in," she said.

Mr. Gordon cleared his throat. "I propose we look into the cost of providing an additional waste pickup to Murphy High," he said. "But that still leaves the cost of the storage containers. If the students are serious about this recycling effort, perhaps they can raise money to buy the bins themselves. By selling candy or some other item, they should have no trouble coming up with the money."

"I'll let the club know," said Sarah, giving her father a grateful smile.

The other members of the school board considered this and agreed to study the matter. After a few more minutes, the school superintendent banged a small gavel and the meeting was over.

Mr. Gordon was beaming as they walked out of the meeting. "You did great in there," he said, giving Sarah a kiss.

"I was scared to death!" said Sarah. "I can't believe Mr. Schlesinger tried to shoot it down."

"He may have helped save it," said Mr. Gordon. "Usually, when students address the school board, their ideas aren't very...realistic. But you presented a strong case, and when Mr. Schlesinger responded, you held your ground. That gave you more authority."

When they reached the car, Mr. Gordon surprised Sarah by getting into the passenger seat. "You get behind the wheel," he told her.

"Oh, Dad, not tonight. I'm still nervous from the meeting."

"Right now," said Mr. Gordon firmly. "It's easy, believe me. It's automatic transmission, so all you have to do is put it in 'Drive,' and then drive!"

Easy for him to say, Sarah thought. Nevertheless, she buckled herself in.

"Aren't you going to buckle up?" she asked.

"No. In case I have to make a sudden grab for the wheel," said Mr. Gordon.

That didn't make Sarah feel any more confident. Mr. Gordon told her to back out of the parking space and go around the building. Sarah did so, moving at what felt like an inch a minute. Even at that slow speed, the car bucked slightly when she hit the brake pedal.

"Don't forget to use your turn signals when we come up to the corners of the building," Mr. Gordon told her. "And relax," he added with a grin.

But Sarah could not relax. She gripped the steering wheel so tightly, her fingers ached. The tight grip made her turns jerky and fast. After a particularly awkward stop, she heard Tasha's clipboard and notes sliding off the backseat. Her father didn't say anything except "You're doing fine," now and then. After twenty minutes, Mr. Gordon told her to park and turn off the car. Sarah did so, then wiped the sweat from her palms on her jacket.

When Mr. Gordon opened the passenger door, he crouched down as if to kiss the ground. "Thank heaven *that's* over!"

"Very funny, Dad."

"Seriously. You did great," Mr. Gordon said, stepping around the car to give her a hug. "You're just going to get better and better, and soon you'll be begging me to let you borrow the car. My girl is growing up." He said it with pride and a little wistfulness.

As they drove home, Sarah looked over at her father. "Dad, I know about Mom's biopsy."

"She told me she was thinking of telling you," he said after a pause. "How long have you known?"

"Since this afternoon. Do you think it's cancer?"

"I don't know. That's the hardest part about all this: not knowing."

"If it's cancer, she could die, right?"

"Absolutely not," said Mr. Gordon firmly. "The worst that would happen is that she would get very sick for a while. But there's no chance she'll die. I don't want you worrying about that, okay?"

Sarah nodded, but she knew her father was just trying to keep her spirits up. "Mom had some pamphlets about breast cancer in the bedroom yesterday. Do you know where they are?"

"Yes, but don't ask me for them. They'll just scare you for no reason."

"Please, Dad. You said the toughest part about all this was not knowing." She felt herself getting angry.

"You can ask your mother for them when we get home," said Mr. Gordon. "Let's not talk about it anymore." He turned on the radio.

Mrs. Gordon was asleep by the time Sarah and her father got home, so Sarah couldn't look for the pamphlets. As scared as she was about the disease, she wanted to know more about it. Tomorrow I'll go to the school library during lunch, she told herself. She was lying on her bed when Tasha walked in.

"How did it go tonight?" Tasha asked, glancing at the clipboard on Sarah's desk.

Sarah told her. When she got to the part about

Mr. Schlesinger, Tasha laughed.

"This morning he gave me grief, and tonight he gives you grief!" said Tasha. She was quiet for a moment, then added, "I felt awful when the two of you left. I really felt I let the club down. And I don't blame your father a bit for being mad." She nudged Sarah's leg playfully. "You're always stepping in to pull my butt out of trouble."

Darn right, thought Sarah. She was glad Tasha had said so. She knew how difficult it was for her cousin to admit her faults.

"I think I called about a hundred people tonight," said Tasha excitedly. "Tomorrow, we're all going to wear something with a kente pattern on it." But Sarah didn't seem to be paying attention. "Are you all right, cuz?"

"No," said Sarah. More than anything, she wanted to share her worries about her mother with Tasha, but she remembered her promise. Finally she said, "Dad let me drive around the parking lot after the meeting."

"All right, Sarah! How was it?"

"So-so. I brake too hard, and sometimes I forget to put on the turn signal."

"It'll come to you," said Tasha as she made her way to Sarah's door. "It's like riding a bicycle: once you learn, you never forget. So, lighten up, girl. You can't let a lousy driving lesson get you so down." She turned off Sarah's light and closed the bedroom door.

"I wish that were it," said Sarah in the dark room.

Five

"As you know, the west side of the building was defaced by soap yesterday," Mr. Schlesinger droned through the P.A. system.

It was Thursday morning, and Sarah and Tasha sat in homeroom. Tasha wore a round hat made of kente cloth, as she had promised.

The students giggled as the vice principal described the Mad Soaper's latest strike. "If anyone knows who is responsible, please contact me at the main office or leave a note in my mailbox. Even though it's only soap, it's still defacement of property and it takes the time of the custodians, who could be working on more important things."

"Sounds to me like the Mad Soaper is *helping* the janitors," Alec Folsom piped up. "If this keeps up, we're going to have the cleanest school in the state!" That brought more chuckles from the class.

After the announcements had been read and the Pledge of Allegiance said, Sarah unfolded *The Murphy Monthly*, which had been slipped into everyone's locker that morning. She usually read the comics first, then "Dear Wally," an advice column addressed to the school's mascot. But this time, Tasha took the newspaper out of her hands and turned to the second page.

"There it is," Tasha said.

Sarah saw her cousin's name, printed in bold type, under a big headline, "Is There Racism in the House?"

Murphy High Rools! That's what the Mad Soaper says, and I agree. But in order for us to stay tight as a school, we can't let racism infect the student body. Recently I have heard jokes that said things like Santa Claus was black because only a black man would wear a red suit. These stories put us down as a race and have no place in school. If you agree, strike a blow against racism! Next time you hear a prejudiced joke, or anything that makes others feel small, don't repeat it. Be brave, and tell the joker that you don't like it. Minorities have it hard enough without having to deal with this. Go Murph!

Sarah looked up at her cousin, who wore a frown on her face.

"I can't believe they printed it on page two!" Tasha said. "That should have been on the front page."

"Good letter," said Brenda Greer, who was also black. "I was there when Rick Hathaway told that joke."

"If you're down with us," Tasha said, "sign the petition that Kwame Brown started. Do you know Kwame?"

"Everybody knows Kwame," said Brenda with a laugh.

"Wait," said Sarah, pulling her copy of the petition out of her backpack, where it had stayed since she had tried to get Rick to sign it.

Brenda signed it in red ink with a flourish that took up another three lines. When a few other classmates approached Tasha to talk about the letter, they signed the petition as well. As she watched Tasha talking to the other students, Sarah felt proud of her. The only thing that bothered her a little was an article on the next page that talked about the Ecology Club. In it, Tasha was mentioned as the member who would speak to the school board about the recycling bins.

I did the work, and she gets the credit, thought Sarah.

"We're going to have a picnic at the soccer field," Tasha told Sarah after third period that morning. "It's a perfect day for it," she said, pointing to the sunshine that streamed into an open classroom.

Sarah shook her head. "I have other plans." She wanted to eat her lunch quickly and head over to the library to read about breast cancer.

"Suit yourself," said Tasha.

Sarah was about to go when Rick approached. Marc Halle was with him, and Marc was wearing a kente cloth hat as well.

Rick waved a copy of *The Murphy Monthly* in his hand. His face was bright red with anger. "Get it through your head, Tasha. I'm not a racist!" he shouted.

The noise in the hallway quieted, and other students turned to look at them. Dave and Kwame heard Rick shouting Tasha's name and hurried over.

Tasha glared at the white junior. "You mean you didn't tell that joke outside the cafeteria doors the other day?"

"It wasn't racist," Rick insisted.

Marc nodded. "Yo, Tasha, why are you trying to stir up trouble where there ain't none?" he said. "Rick and I grew up together. He can tell me any black joke he wants, and I can tell him any white joke I want. The rest is none of your business."

"It's my business," said Tasha, "if I hear it, and I get offended."

"Well, maybe you're too sensitive; did you ever think about that?" said a white girl standing behind Rick.

"Hey, all I wrote was that we should fight racism," said Tasha. "If you're not racist, then you've got nothing to worry about."

"I've got plenty to worry about," Rick shot back. "Everyone knew who you were talking about in that letter."

The crowd of observers had thickened, and Sarah could hear separate arguments splintering off between black and white students. She glanced at Kwame, who was trying to reason with an angry white student.

"This is crazy," muttered Tasha. She tried to make

her way through the crowd, but Rick grabbed her by the arm. "Don't touch me!" cried Tasha, her eyes blazing.

Rick pulled his hand back quickly. "I want to settle this once and for all. You made me out to be some kind of redneck bigot."

"You did that yourself," Tasha replied. Kwame and a few other students loudly agreed.

"Hey! Listen up!" said Dave. The crowd quieted down a bit. "You two are never going to agree on this, so stop shouting at each other!" He pointed to Tasha. "You think it's hate speech, and Rick, you think it's freedom of speech."

"If you would just listen to me for two minutes, I could prove you are overreacting," said Rick.

"And I could prove you're insensitive to minorities," said Tasha. Her response brought forth a new wave of yells and threats.

"You two should hold a debate," said Kwame.

"Fine by me," said Tasha. "But if I win, you have to apologize for your prejudiced joke. In public. In the school paper."

"And if I win," said Rick vehemently, "you have to write another letter in *The Murphy Monthly* in which you state my joke wasn't racist, and you were being too sensitive. Because that's what you are!"

"We'll see about that" was all Tasha said.

The bell rang, and those in the crowd who had wanted to see a fight hurried off. But Rick, Tasha, and a few others stayed. They agreed to hold the debate after school next Thursday in the activities lounge. Mr. Cintron, a social studies teacher, would be the moderator.

Once Rick had left, Kwame turned to Tasha. "This is going to be great," he said with a big grin.

Tasha threw a few punches in the air like a boxer in training. "I'll knock him out in the first round, Coach," she told Kwame. Then she turned to her cousin. "Don't worry, Sarah. This is one speech you won't have to give for me."

18 PINE

Six

"If you lose, you're going to have to apologize to him," said Jennifer Wilson at 18 Pine St. later that day. "Are you willing to do that?"

"Yes," said Tasha. "But I won't have to."

Sarah listened to her cousin talk about the debate. She was glad for her cousin, but her mind was on her mother's health. The article she had read in the library about breast cancer had made her even more nervous about her mother's condition. It did not help to learn that black women were more likely to die than white women because they tended to put off breast exams, nor was she happy to hear that the disease ran in some families. "*If* it is cancer," she kept telling herself.

Sarah walked to the pay phone near the rest rooms of the pizza shop and dialed her mother's office.

"The lab hasn't called me yet, honey," said Mrs. Gordon.

"How do you feel?"

"A little worried."

As Sarah hung up, she found herself wishing her mother had lied to her and said she was fine.

José, Kwame, and Robert had joined the group when Sarah returned to the booth. Billy grabbed a nearby table and set it next to the booth to make more room. Cindy and Julie came in moments later.

The news of the upcoming debate seemed to have lifted the strain that Sarah had noticed among her friends in the past few days. No one except Tasha seemed particularly eager to discuss the joke, or Tasha's article in the school newspaper that morning, and that was fine by Sarah.

"Check this out, everybody," said Steve when he came in. He unfolded a bundle of plastic into what looked like a large pyramid.

"What is *that*, some kind of kite?" said Jennifer. "Aren't you a little old to be flying kites?"

"It's a Tetra Kite," Steve informed her. "It was invented by Alexander Graham Bell. You've got to wear gloves when you fly this thing if you want to be safe. It has a lot of pull, and the line can cut your hand if you're not careful."

"What fun is that?" Jennifer mumbled.

"What fun is shopping at the mall?" Steve countered.

"Ooh," said José, "that hit her where she lives." Everyone knew how much Jennifer loved to shop.

"Different strokes for different folks, right?" said Dave.

Tasha helped herself to one of Billy's french fries. "You're still going to take me driving tonight, aren't you?" she whispered.

"Sure," said Billy. "But I thought you'd be staying home and getting ready for that debate."

"I'm prepared right now," said Tasha. She pulled out the petition Kwame had started. "Check this out," she said to the group. "Everyone who signed this is on my side. All Rick has is Marc Halle, and a few white boys who don't want to back down."

Jennifer shook her head. "I'd be careful if I was you, Tasha. Rick is a good speaker. He's in our history class," she said, pointing to Sarah and Dave, "and when Mrs. Parisi splits us up to take sides on something, his side usually wins."

"I'll bet he takes the side of the South when the Civil War comes up!" Kwame murmured.

"Big deal," said Tasha. "I've got Kwame to help me. And," she added mischievously, "I've got a secret weapon. My aunt is a lawyer, right? Well, I'm going to ask her to take Rick's part in the debate. Then I can practice my arguments against her. If I can hold my own, I'll have no problem next week."

"That's great!" said Kwame. He rubbed his hands together and cackled like a mad scientist.

Robert lifted his soda can in a toast. "May you beat the pants off him!" he said.

"You know, I'm surprised at you, Robert," said Sarah. "You love telling jokes, but you can't see anything funny in this one. Why is that?"

65

"I don't have trouble with jokes about blacks," said Robert, "if they're told by blacks. But I think Rick went too far. Trouble is, everyone has a different idea about what 'too far' is."

"Then why can't you admit that Rick has a different limit than you do and leave it at that?" Steve asked Robert.

Kwame answered for him. "Because when you tell a fat joke, you don't tell it in front of someone who's fat and who might feel bad about it," he said.

Billy took off his sunglasses and gave Kwame a look of distaste. "Listen, Kwame, some people complain that football is too violent. I'll listen to their arguments, but do you think they're going to convince me not to play? Uh-uh," he said, shaking his head. "Just because someone can't handle what you're doing, doesn't mean you stop doing it—you know what I'm saying? That's where Rick has a point."

"But Rick's joke disrespected me as a black person," said Kwame.

"If one measly joke threatens your black identity, maybe you're too insecure," said Billy.

"Exactly," said Steve.

"Stay out of this, Steve. You have nothing to say about this," said Jennifer.

"He's got a right to his opinion," Cindy told Jennifer.

A bunch of heated arguments seemed to erupt at once. Steve accused Kwame of not having a sense of humor. Jennifer argued with Cindy about whether light-skinned blacks had it easier than dark-skinned blacks.

Sarah found herself listening to Robert as he argued with Julie.

"I wonder how Rick would feel if someone picked on him for being white," said Robert.

"Are you going to tell him some anti-white joke?" asked Julie.

"Maybe he'd be a lot more aware of race if he got a taste of his own medicine, that's all," said Robert.

"What do you have in mind?" said Dave.

"I don't have anything in mind," Robert said. He tugged at his rugby shirt absently and took a long drink of his soda.

April had been very quiet as she watched her friends argue back and forth. Finally, she spoke up, trying to break the tension. "So, Sarah. Is your mother pregnant or isn't she?"

Tasha gave April an incredulous look. Then she turned her gaze toward Sarah.

"It . . . I think it was just the flu or something."

"What about those tests she had taken?" she said.

By now, all eyes were on Sarah. But she felt Tasha's gaze most intently. "Just routine woman's stuff tests," Sarah replied casually. "I don't want to go into details with men around."

"On behalf of the men," said Billy, holding up his root beer cup, "thank you!"

"Yeah," said Robert with a chuckle. "I took health last semester, and one thing I learned is, you all got some complicated plumbing!"

Robert expected a big laugh, and he got a few half-hearted ones from Billy and Dave, but the girls gave him icy looks. His eyes widened when he saw Cindy's angry expression.

"You talk about being sensitive," she said, jabbing Robert in the chest with a finger. "Then you go and talk about my body like it's a house!"

"I was just kidding," said Robert feebly.

"See?" said Billy triumphantly. "Rick said he was kidding, too, but noooo."

Steve chuckled. "Hey Robert, maybe you should debate the girls about this."

Kwame gave Steve a serious look. "I don't think Rick's situation is the same thing. Robert may have crossed the line, but that's just Robert."

"You'd better make sure you prepare for that debate," Dave told Tasha. "Jennifer was right about Rick: he's good."

"He's good, but I'm right," said Tasha.

Billy couldn't help laughing at that. "If this is how you take a joke about a red suit, I'd hate to be around you when something *really* racist comes up."

"I wasn't talking to you, Billy," Tasha snapped. "And I don't think you should talk to me until you can learn to respect my feelings."

"Does that mean the driving lesson is off?" said Billy sarcastically.

"*You and I* are off," said Tasha. "And it's going to stay that way until you find some manners around me." She grabbed her jacket and book bag and headed for the door.

"That's right! You and I are off," Billy called after her. "It's going to be off until you learn to pick your battles." He turned back to the table. "I'm not less of a black person just because I don't find a racist under every rock."

Steve stood up and put on his jacket. He picked up his kite and left the table without saying a word.

"Good riddance," said Kwame under his breath.

José gave Kwame a shocked look. "You were his best friend, man." He looked around the table, then stood up in disgust. "Somebody call me when you all get tired of acting like *niños!*" he said, using the Spanish word that meant children.

Sarah was the next to go. "I've got to see about Tasha," she said. Outside, she spied Tasha heading up Pine Street.

"You passed the bus stop," said Sarah, catching up.

"I'll catch it farther down the line," Tasha murmured. "Why don't you go back and get a ride with Dave?"

"I'll walk awhile with you, if you don't mind."

"I'm not in the mood to talk," said Tasha. Still, she slowed down so that Sarah could fall in step.

In her mind, Sarah kept seeing her group of close friends bickering with each other. How could people who spent so much time together react so differently to the same event? she asked herself. Sarah stole a look at Tasha and wondered what she was thinking. But it was impossible to know what was going on under that kente cloth hat.

Seven

The Ecology Club met in Mr. Rowland's biology room that Friday afternoon. Tasha had refused to attend, telling Sarah she had to prepare for the debate. But Sarah suspected it had more to do with her cousin's pride. Tasha didn't want to be there when Sarah gave the school board report she had promised to give herself.

"It's up to us," Sarah told the club. "If we can come up with the money to buy the recycling bins, they'll find the money for an extra waste pickup."

"All right," said Mr. Rowland. "Let's have some money-making ideas."

"We could hold a raffle," suggested one club member.

"What would we raffle off?" Sarah asked. No one could think of anything, and the idea died right there.

"We can sell Hershey bars or some other candy," said Tammy, a girl who wore her red hair in a crew cut.

"I'm lousy at selling," said a boy in the back.

"Then you can buy some!" said Tammy. The group quickly voted for the idea, and Mr. Rowland promised to order the candy right away.

"In the meantime, we can still sell," said Mr. Rowland. "I'm going to be chaperoning the Battle of the Bands next Tuesday. The Yearbook Club is already selling orange drink there, but we can set up a table with cookies and such."

When the meeting broke up, Sarah had volunteered to bake two pans of brownies to sell at the band competition.

"Peanut butter or tuna fish?" Sarah called out to Julie and Cindy. It was Sunday afternoon, and the three friends had just returned from the Westcove Mall.

"Peanut butter," they said.

Cindy took off her sneaker and massaged her foot. "We must have walked five miles in that mall!"

"And we never did find the nail polish to match this," said Julie, holding up a lipstick applicator in a purple hue.

"I bet Jennifer would have found it," said Cindy quietly. Jennifer rarely missed a chance to go shopping with her friends, but that morning she had made it clear that she didn't want to hang around with Cindy or anyone else who didn't agree with Tasha and Kwame about Rick's insensitivity.

Sarah finished making the sandwiches and poured three glasses of Kool-Aid before joining her friends at the small kitchen table. Her feet also ached, but she was in a good mood. Yesterday, Mrs. Gordon had called the doctor to inquire about the results of her test. It turned out the hospital had misplaced the report, but they immediately put a tracer on the file. Mr. Gordon had taken the news as a good sign. "They wouldn't have been so careless if they had found something serious," he said.

Cindy was telling Sarah a funny story about her Jamaican grandfather when Julie returned from the bathroom. "Is your grandmother going off to do another commercial?" she asked.

"If she is, I don't know about it," said Sarah and gave her a quizzical look. "Why do you ask?"

"I saw her putting a suitcase out in the hall," said Julie.

It wasn't the usual overnight bag that Miss Essie took to auditions, Sarah noticed when she climbed the stairs. The suitcase came from her mother's luggage set. Miss Essie appeared in the doorway of Mrs. Gordon's bedroom. Her eyes were pink, and her cheeks glittered with two lines of tears.

Sarah went into the room and closed the door behind her. Her mother was crying on the far edge of the bed, but she wiped away her tears as soon as Sarah appeared.

"Mom, what is it?" asked Sarah. Her stomach was in knots.

"Come here, baby," Mrs. Gordon whispered. She hugged Sarah very tightly, then held her at arm's length and gazed directly into her daughter's eyes. "I want you to be brave for me, okay?"

Sarah stared at her mother, unable to say anything.

"Sarah, the hospital called while you were out . . . It's cancer."

Sarah flung her arms around her mother. "Oh no!" she sobbed. "No!"

Tasha had been shooting baskets in the driveway when Sarah returned from the mall with her two friends. Now she was surprised to see Julie and Cindy coming out of the house and hurrying toward her, their faces grim.

"Something's wrong," said Julie. "Sarah went upstairs a few minutes ago, and she never came back down. We heard her crying."

"Tell her we went home, okay?" said Cindy.

Tasha ran inside. She found Sarah in Mrs. Gordon's bedroom, curled on the bed like a little child. Miss Essie sat on the vanity chair, dabbing her eyes with a balled-up tissue. Mrs. Gordon told Tasha about the cancer, but the news didn't seem real to her. Tasha hugged her aunt for a long time, then sat at the edge of the bed feeling slightly dazed. Her little cousin, Allison, came in a few moments later and began to cry without waiting for anyone to tell her what was wrong. Tasha wondered why she felt detached from the scene, as if she were watching a movie.

"My surgery is scheduled for Monday morning," Mrs. Gordon told them during a lull in the crying. "That's tomorrow. The procedure is called a lumpectomy." She gave them a weak smile. "Strange name, isn't it?"

"Are they going to remove your breast?" Sarah asked.

"No. That's called a mastectomy," her mother told her. "If they don't get it all in this operation, they might have to remove the whole breast, yes."

"Where's Daddy now?" Allison asked.

"He's at the hospital. He's donating blood for my operation." The news brought forth a new round of sobs from Allison.

"What do you want us to do, Mom?" said Sarah.

"I want you to think positive about this like I am," said Mrs. Gordon. "This year, a hundred and sixty thousand women will be diagnosed with breast cancer, but if it's caught early enough, the chances of survival are excellent. I have a feeling I'll be just fine. But in the meantime, you kids are going to have to keep one another's spirits up."

They heard Mr. Gordon's car pulling into the driveway. He appeared in the bedroom doorway still wearing his jacket and hat. Mr. Gordon kissed his wife on the forehead, then hugged each of the girls before finding a spot on the king-sized bed.

"Your mother will go to the hospital tonight so they can do some tests and prepare her for the operation," he told them. "She'll probably be in the hospital for a few days after that to make sure the entire tumor was removed. I'm going to be there a lot of the time, so I want you to do everything Miss Essie tells you with no backtalk, is that clear?"

"I've already talked to them, Donald," said Mrs. Gordon soothingly. "Now if you'll all get out of my way," she said, rising from the bed, "I don't want to spend this beautiful day in bed. I've got to make a list of things I have to take care of here, and at the office."

Everyone left the bedroom except Allison, who refused to move away from her mother's side. Sarah walked down the stairs, feeling numb. She put on her coat and walked into the backyard. She stared at the square patch of earth where Mr. Gordon planted every year. The ground was mucky and bare, except where a few early weeds were pushing through. She heard the door opening behind her, and Tasha appeared behind the screen door.

"They could be wrong," said Tasha. There was a hollow ring to her voice.

"What do you mean?"

Tasha sat next to Sarah and shrugged. "I mean, they could have made a mistake. Your mom told me the hospital lost the test results for two days. Well, what if they got them mixed up or something?"

"It's cancer!" said Sarah. "Why do you think Dad was at the hospital?"

Tasha got up. "It could be a mistake," she said firmly. She walked across the grass and disappeared around the side of the house. Moments later, Sarah heard her cousin shooting baskets in the driveway.

Is the news so bad that Tasha simply refuses to accept it? she wondered.

She picked up a stick and threw it at the garden plot.

She remembered the night she had spoken to her father about the tumor. "The worst part is not knowing," Mr. Gordon had said.

"The worst part is *knowing*!" she mumbled as fresh tears sprang to her eyes.

PINE

Eight

That evening, while Mrs. Gordon was making last-minute arrangements before leaving for the hospital, Sarah went out to the driveway to talk to her father. She found him putting Mrs. Gordon's suitcase in the trunk of the car.

"How are you holding up?" Mr. Gordon asked her.

"I'm fine, I guess. I'm worried about Tasha. It's like she doesn't believe what's happening with Mom," said Sarah.

Mr. Gordon looked up at Tasha's bedroom window on the second floor. There were no lights on in the room, but there was faint music coming from a radio. "I can't imagine what she's going through right now," he said. "First she lost her parents, and now her aunt is . . ." He let the words trail off. "Maybe we should have told her about the tumor, the way we told you, so she would have been ready for this possibility."

"Why didn't you?" said Sarah.

"She's gone through a lot of pain for someone who's only sixteen," said Mr. Gordon. "We were afraid it would be too much for her."

Mrs. Gordon appeared in the doorway and announced she was ready. Allison insisted on coming to the hospital to see her off. When Sarah ran upstairs for her coat, she knocked on Tasha's door.

"We're going to the hospital. Are you coming?"

"No," said Tasha through the door.

Miss Essie came up to Sarah in the hallway. "You-all go on," she said. "I'll stay here with Tasha."

On Monday morning, Dave Hunter appeared at the kitchen door. "Mom saw your dad at the hospital yesterday," he said. "She told me everything. I'm really sorry."

"Thanks," said Sarah, giving him a hug. She had slept fitfully the night before, and her body was heavy with fatigue.

"Anyway, Mom let me have the car, in case you want a lift to school," said Dave.

When Tasha came down a few minutes later, she greeted Dave brightly and acted as if everything were fine. But from the look in her cousin's eyes, Sarah could tell that Tasha, too, had slept poorly.

They were driving through downtown Madison when Dave suddenly pulled the car to the curb. "Wait here," he said. He disappeared into a drugstore and returned with a huge Snoopy get-well card.

"We'll get the gang to sign it," he said.

They got to the school just as Billy was walking across the students' parking lot. Tasha was carrying the big card. "Is that card for me?" he called out. "You come to apologize for the way you've been acting?"

Before Tasha could say anything, Dave told Billy what the card was for.

Billy looked very embarrassed and mumbled an apology. "Let me sign it," he said, looking for a pen inside his duffel bag.

As they entered the school, Sarah's eye fell on a red and gold banner hanging from the window in the activities lounge. "Battle of the Bands!" it read. Underneath the letters was a picture of two cartoon guitars slugging it out in a boxing ring. She and Dave had made plans to go, and she had also promised the Ecology Club two trays of brownies to sell.

"I'm not going," said Sarah. She gave Dave an apologetic look. "Tomorrow is the first day I can visit my mom," she explained. Dave gave her a look that said their date for the band contest was the last thing she should worry about.

Most of Sarah and Tasha's friends had heard about Mrs. Gordon's condition by lunchtime. Even some of the teachers knew about the operation. Mr. Cala had taken Tasha aside and informed her that he would give her more time to turn in her homework.

Sarah smiled gratefully at the table of friends who had signed the card at lunch. "My mom will really appreciate this," she said.

"There's some people missing," said Kwame when he looked at the names in the card. "Steve and José still haven't signed." He looked around the cafeteria, then spied the two of them playing Hacky Sack in the courtyard.

When Steve saw his former friend approaching, he scowled. "What do *you* want?" he said. "Does the way I kick a Hacky Sack offend you?"

"Sarah's mother is in the hospital, and we've got a card we want everyone to sign," said Kwame.

Steve flushed a bright pink. He and José followed Kwame back to the cafeteria. The card lay open in the middle of the table, but what drew their attention was the sight of Tasha sobbing uncontrollably. Billy was holding her in his arms, and Sarah was on her other side, stroking her hair.

"What happened?" José asked April in a whisper.

April looked scared. Her blue eyes were also filled with tears. "I don't know," she said. "One minute she was fine, talking about the debate this Thursday, and the next thing, she was crying."

"I'm fine," said Tasha after a moment. She seemed embarrassed by the attention she had drawn, and pulled away from Billy. "I just need a drink of water."

"I'll get it," said Billy. "You just sit there."

"No, I want to go myself." Tasha stood up and headed toward the doors that led to the library. Sarah was right behind her.

"You going to be all right?" said Sarah as Tasha took a long drink from the fountain in the hallway.

Tasha stared at her shoes. "I'm a bad person, Sarah," she said in a shaky voice. "I should have gone to the hospital last night with your mom. I shouldn't have snuck off to go driving with Billy. I should have done my duty to the Ecology Club." She pointed toward the cafeteria. "And now my friends are fighting with each other because of me and Rick."

Sarah gave her cousin's shoulder a gentle shake. "Stop it, Tasha. You're not a bad person. Nobody hates you for not going to the hospital last night. And the Ecology Club couldn't care less which one of us went to that meeting. And maybe our friends don't see eye to eye right now, but if one fight breaks the group apart, then it wasn't much to begin with."

"I can't wait for this stupid debate to be over," said Tasha.

Sarah found a clean tissue in her pocket and gave it to Tasha, whose eyes were tearing up again. "That's another thing," said Sarah. "You are in no condition to be worrying about a debate. When I see Rick in history class today, I'm going to call it off."

"No!" said Tasha vehemently. The sadness in her eyes was gone, replaced by a determined look.

"Well, then at least let me postpone it," said Sarah. "We've got more important things to worry about this week."

Tasha thought about this. "All right," she said finally. "But don't tell him why. I don't want his pity."

Sarah saw Rick in her history class that afternoon and told him the news. "Something came up, so Tasha won't be ready for the debate on Thursday."

Rick grinned and spread his hands apart in a gesture of generosity. "Hey, if she needs more time to get ready, that's fine with me. What about next Tuesday? Will she be ready then?"

Sarah assured him Tasha would be.

Nine

On Tuesday, the Gordon cousins found Mr. Gordon in the Murphy High parking lot, waiting to take them to Madison County Hospital. When they arrived at Mrs. Gordon's room, Miss Essie and Allison were already there.

"She's sleeping," said Sarah's grandmother.

Sarah looked at her mother asleep on the bed. A tube that led to a bottle of clear fluid was attached to the top of her hand.

A tall Indian doctor came in to check on his patient. "The operation went very well," he told the Gordon family.

"Did they get it all?" Sarah asked him. She knew from her library reading that sometimes more than one operation was necessary to remove all the cancer.

"We can't be sure until we observe her for the next few days," he said. "Then we'll have to perform a second biopsy. But I think—" He was interrupted by a cry from Allison.

"Mom!" said Allison.

Mrs. Gordon had awakened. She saw her family around her and smiled.

"How are you feeling?" asked the doctor.

"Fine," whispered Mrs. Gordon.

"In that case, I'd better go find someone sick to look after," said the doctor with a smile. He left the room to the Gordons.

After everyone had gotten a chance to hug Mrs. Gordon, Sarah handed her the card Dave had bought. Her mother read all the wishes and told Sarah to thank everyone for it.

"She looked good," said Tasha as they rode home with Miss Essie an hour later.

"She's in great spirits," Miss Essie agreed.

They hadn't been home a minute before the doorbell rang. Sarah opened it to find Dave's mother smiling at her. Next to Mrs. Hunter stood two women Sarah had never seen before. All three of them held casserole dishes covered with foil.

"Don't just stand there, child, let them in," said Miss Essie, appearing behind her.

Sarah accepted the casseroles and took her time placing them in the refrigerator. She didn't feel like talking to Mrs. Hunter and her friends, and decided to stay in the kitchen. She overheard them talking with Miss Essie about all sorts of diseases, and how long it took to recover from them. She stayed in the kitchen as long as she could, coming out only when Miss Essie asked her to make a pot of coffee for the guests. It proved to be a mistake. Mrs. Hunter took her hand and asked her how she was holding up, how Tasha was coping with it, and how Allison was taking it.

When she could stand it no longer, Sarah excused herself and told the women she had homework to do.

"Are they still down there?" Tasha asked when Sarah walked past her room.

"Yeah," Sarah answered. She found Tasha sitting at her desk, doodling in a sketchbook.

"I'll bet they brought tuna casserole and three-bean salad."

Sarah laughed. "That's right! How did you know?"

Tasha made a face and continued doodling in her sketchbook. "After my mom and dad died, I went to live with Aunt Elise for a while, and the ladies at her church brought me all sorts of food I didn't like."

Sarah shrugged. "I guess it's just their way of saying they care."

"It's their way of meddling!" Tasha retorted. "The last thing I cared about when my parents died was eating tuna casserole! Aunt Elise's friends brought food by just to have an excuse to see how I was holding up. Just so they could tell other people. Phonies!"

Sarah was surprised to hear herself defending the women downstairs. "Mrs. Hunter is not a phony. She really cares about us."

Tasha pursed her lips and bit back the urge to sob. "I've seen those women too many times in my life," she said.

"I'll bet you have," said Sarah softly. She hugged her cousin. A second later, she sensed Tasha crying silently on her shoulder, and Sarah held her tighter.

That night, Sarah had trouble sleeping. After tossing and turning in the bed, she finally got up for a drink of water. She was surprised to hear faint radio music coming from Tasha's doorway. She knocked on her cousin's door and heard the radio go off.

"You couldn't sleep either, huh?" Tasha asked when Sarah entered the room.

"Nope," said Sarah. She sat at Tasha's desk, and the two of them talked softly by the light of the streetlamp seeping in through the window.

"What are you guys doing in here?" said Allison from the doorway. Tasha motioned her cousin onto her bed.

"We couldn't sleep," said Tasha.

"Me neither. Are you guys scared about Mom?" Allison asked.

"A little," Sarah admitted. "But I think she's going to be all right. I really do."

Allison seemed to take comfort from this. "If Mom makes it," she vowed, "I'm going to do everything she tells me, and not cause her any trouble."

"Wow, you *are* scared," said Tasha. They all smiled.

"What's going on in here? What are you doing up?" said Miss Essie, startling the girls.

"We're just talking, Miss Essie," Tasha whispered.

Their grandmother left momentarily and returned from her room with a candle, which she placed on Tasha's desk and lit with a lighter. Then she motioned Allison to move over, and sat down at the foot of the bed. "Now, then: what are we going to talk about?"

They talked about Mrs. Gordon.

"Is she going to lose her hair?" Allison asked.

"It's possible," Miss Essie admitted. "The medicine they use to fight cancer is very strong, and sometimes it makes the hair fall out."

When Tasha brought up the subject of Mrs. Hunter and her snooping church friends, Miss Essie asked her to be understanding. "When they were here this evening, they bowed their heads and prayed for your aunt to get better," she said. "If that's 'meddling,' I'll take it any day of the week."

They watched the candlelight flickering over the bedroom walls and on each other's faces and talked softly into the night. Miss Essie talked about what Mr. and Mrs. Gordon were like before Sarah was born, then amused them with stories about Sarah's father and Tasha's father. "Those two boys fought like crazy with each other," said Miss Essie. "But the minute somebody from the outside threatened one brother, the other was right there to defend him." She paused for a moment, then pointed to Allison, who had been quiet for some time. They saw she had fallen asleep on the bed.

"I'm fading fast, too," said Miss Essie, stifling a yawn. "Oh my gosh, it's one thirty-four!" she said, looking at the digital clock on the nightstand. They had been talking for over an hour. Miss Essie said good night and guided her youngest granddaughter back to her room, taking the candle with her. "Don't stay up much longer," she told Sarah and Tasha.

When Allison and her grandmother were gone, Tasha let out a soft laugh. "That was almost like a slumber party."

"Yeah, I think we should do it again with Mom when she gets better," said Sarah. "*When* she gets better, not *if*," she added firmly.

"That's right, 'when, not if,'" said Tasha, just as confidently.

Ten

"It's not the same without everyone here," Kwame told Robert Thornton. It was Tuesday night, and the boys were at the Battle of the Bands. It seemed as if the Gordon cousins weren't the only two friends who had decided to stay away.

Kwame wandered around the gym wearing his best pair of baggy black slacks, with a blue and green striped shirt that fell, untucked, past his pants pockets. Robert Thornton had dressed up a little more, wearing khaki pants, a blue blazer, and a loosely knotted tie over a pale yellow shirt.

"Let's stay out here until they're done," said Robert, gesturing impatiently at the punk rock band playing inside the gym just then. A lot of the grown-ups who were chaperoning the event seemed to have the same idea.

"What's up, guys?" said Billy when he spied them by

the drinking fountain.

"This show is a bust," said Robert scornfully. "The bands were much better last year."

"Not only that," said Kwame bitterly, "but the Ecology Club ran out of cookies and brownies fifteen minutes ago, and the orange drink machine the Yearbook Club was running just broke down."

Billy and Robert looked at each other before breaking into laughter.

"Maybe we should call it the Battle of the Snacks, eh, Kwame?" said Billy.

Before Kwame could respond, the three were distracted by the sound of someone trying to open one of the building's side entrances.

"You got to go around," said Robert to the person outside. Just then, Wayne Leatham, the tall, heavyset senior who hung around with Rick Hathaway, came toward them.

"Can't you see someone is trying to get in?" said Wayne, slurring his words a bit. He pushed open the side door, letting in two white girls wearing matching denim jackets and a lot of makeup.

"It's about time," said one of the girls.

"Don't worry, guys, I already paid your admission," said Wayne smugly. The girls laughed and pushed their way past Kwame and his friends. Before turning to follow the girls, Wayne gave Kwame a triumphant grin.

"I heard Rick's got Tasha on the run," he said.

Kwame backed away from the smell of alcohol that came from Wayne's breath. "Tasha will take him apart."

"Then why did she beg for another week to get ready?" said Wayne. "Yeah, she was talking a big game last week, and now it's 'I need more time, Rick,'" he said in a falsetto voice.

Billy didn't like anyone making fun of Tasha, but he especially didn't want to hear it from Wayne. "Why don't you go be with your girls?" he said, struggling to keep his temper.

Wayne was just drunk enough to ignore the menace in Billy's voice. "I was talking to Kwame," Wayne said, turning back to the bespectacled sophomore. "Face it, you people are always asking for special favors."

The words had hardly left his mouth when he found himself shoved against the wall by Robert Thornton.

"You don't know when to shut up, do you?" Robert shouted.

"Don't start anything," said Kwame, stealing a look around the corner. Robert's shout had been heard by one of the chaperones, a muscular gym teacher, who was heading toward them.

Billy tried putting his football player's build between Robert and Wayne, but the two grappling boys didn't release each other. Wayne swung hard, landing a punch on Robert's shoulder, and the fight was on.

"That's enough," said the gym teacher. Two other grown-ups hurried over to give him a hand in separating the fighters. By then, a crowd of students had converged around Wayne and Robert. When they were finally separated, the chaperones discussed whether they should call the police.

"I'll get Robert out of here," Billy told the grown-ups. "You don't have to call the police. We'll just take him home, right, Kwame?"

Kwame nodded.

"I'm not done with you, Robert," Wayne hissed as the two boys were escorted to their cars.

"Any time," said Robert.

Out in the parking lot, a light rain was falling. Kwame and Billy watched as the gym teacher guided Wayne—and the two girls he had snuck into the concert—back to his Camaro. Another man led Robert to his car.

As he drove past Robert, Wayne lowered his window and shouted a vulgar racial slur.

Robert shouted one back at him.

Wayne pointed to Robert's blazer and khaki pants. "What's the matter, homeboy? Is your red suit at the cleaners?" He laughed and gunned the car's engine before he sped off.

Eleven

The morning after the Battle of the Bands concert, Murphy High students found a police car parked in front of the school building. From their school bus, Sarah, Tasha, and Cindy could see two officers standing by the side of the building. The police were trying to keep a growing crowd of students behind a strip of yellow plastic tape that ran five feet out from a section of the school's brick wall.

"What's going on?" said Cindy, as they got off the bus.

"They're pointing at something on the wall," said Sarah. "Maybe the Mad Soaper went too far this time."

When they got close enough to see, Sarah felt a sinking sensation in her stomach. Three letters had been spray-painted on the dark red brick: KKK.

"All right," said Mr. Schlesinger to the crowd of students. "We're going to find out who did this. Stay behind the tape! The police have blocked off the area because we think we might have a footprint, so please stay back. This kind of thing has no place at Murphy. No place."

In homeroom, Mr. Schlesinger repeated over the P.A. system what everyone already knew: someone had spray-painted the initials of the Ku Klux Klan on the wall.

Brenda Greer walked over to the table where Tasha and Sarah sat and asked the question that had been in the back of Sarah's mind all morning. "Do you think Rick and his friends did it?"

"If he didn't, he helped make it possible," said Tasha fiercely. "I'm going to ask him as soon as homeroom is over." Brenda said she would join her, and by the time the bell rang, Tasha led twelve students to Rick's locker.

When Rick saw Tasha and the others, he held up his hands. "I know what you're thinking, but it wasn't me! I don't know who it was!"

"Prove it," shouted Brenda.

"If he said he didn't do it, he didn't do it," said Wayne, pushing his way through the group to stand next to his friend. "Get back."

"It could have been you," said Kwame, who had joined the group. "Do you remember what you yelled at me last night?" He repeated the words Wayne had shouted, and a few students gasped.

Rick looked at Wayne. "Did you really say that?"

Wayne pretended he hadn't heard Rick's question. He

pointed to Kwame. "I didn't do it, either. Maybe you and Robert did it to try to frame me!"

"That's twisted!" said Tasha. Brenda Greer began to shout at Wayne, and Wayne shouted back at her. Rick took advantage of the distraction to work his way past the crowd and sprint down the hallway.

When Sarah and Tasha went to the hospital that Wednesday afternoon, they told Mrs. Gordon about the "KKK" spray-painted on the wall.

"It's hard to believe some student at Murphy has that kind of hate inside him," said Mrs. Gordon sadly. But when Tasha told her aunt about Rick's joke—and blamed him for the vandalism—Mrs. Gordon shook her head. "A boy who wants to settle this matter with a debate doesn't strike me as a spray-paint vandal."

"Maybe not, but whoever did it probably felt bolder because Rick was fighting for his right to tell racist jokes," said Tasha.

"That racist already had the hate inside him," said Mrs. Gordon. "Maybe your argument with Rick brought it out, but at least it's in the open where we can fight it."

They were silent for a moment as the Gordon cousins thought about this.

Sarah had had enough of the subject. She pointed at the bandage on her mother's chest. "How do you feel? Are you in pain?"

"No," said Mrs. Gordon. "The doctors gave me a pain patch." She pointed to a round white disk taped to her shoulder. "It sends painkillers directly into my system."

"When are you coming home?" asked Tasha.

"I don't know, honey," said Mrs. Gordon. "They want to do a few more tests on me. The doctor told me we're halfway there."

"Only halfway!" Sarah cried.

Mrs. Gordon took her hand. "They removed the tumor, but they also had to remove the lymph glands under my left arm. If the cancer got to those glands, it could have spread all over my body." She pointed to an array of orange bottles on the nightstand. "After I leave the hospital, I still have to take some powerful chemicals to kill any cancer that may be lingering inside."

"And *then* you'll be healed?" Tasha asked.

Mrs. Gordon's eyes turned moist. "Yes. But once you get breast cancer, you have a higher risk of getting it again in the other breast. I'm only telling you so it doesn't come as a surprise if it returns."

"I don't want to know anymore!" said Sarah, pressing her hands to her ears and shaking her head. Her tears were flowing freely now. Mrs. Gordon gave her a tissue and took one for herself.

That Thursday, during Sarah's gym class, Mr. Schlesinger made a special announcement: the final class period would be canceled so that the students could attend an assembly. He also announced that the police had finished looking for clues, and the offensive "KKK" letters would be gone by that afternoon. A round of applause broke out among the girls in the gym class.

"Do you think it was the Mad Soaper?" April wondered aloud at lunch that day. "Up until now, he didn't do anything mean, and he never used spray paint."

"It could have been someone who wanted to pin it on the Mad Soaper," Dave proposed.

"I'll bet you anything it was Wayne Leatham," said Billy. "The dude was half drunk at the Battle of the Bands, and he was saying racist things."

"Why don't you tell Mr. Schlesinger about it?" asked Tasha.

"I don't have any proof," said Billy. "And if I send Wayne to the principal's office, he'll tell Schlesinger that I fought with him, and then I'll get in trouble."

"I heard the cops made a plaster cast of a footprint they found in front of the wall," Kwame said. "They ought to do like in Cinderella, and fit that plaster cast on the foot of every white boy in this school!"

Everyone agreed.

At two-fifteen, the entire Murphy High student body filed into the auditorium. Mr. Schlesinger addressed them from the stage.

"There has been a lot of tension in the air here at Murphy in the past week," the vice principal said. "We have invited a group of actors to the school to talk about prejudice. I want you to give them your full attention."

"Wake me up when it's over," Jennifer Wilson murmured to Sarah.

With a crash of cymbals, the stage went dark. A bright spotlight hit the stage, and a handsome black man called out to the Murphy High crowd, "What's up, Murphy? What's up? What's up?"

"Oh my gosh, he's gorgeous!" Jennifer whispered.

A drum machine beat out an infectious rhythm as the actor spoke. "Yo, listen up. My name is Michael, and me and my crew are here to entertain you. I hope you have some fun, and enjoy yourselves." The lights came on all across the stage, and three other men and two women appeared, singing a song called "It's All About Respect." Sarah smiled. It was a little corny, she thought, but it was funny, too.

"If you don't respect yourself, and if you don't respect others, what are you going to end up?" Michael cried.

"A nothing!" said one of the men.

"A nobody!" cried one of the women.

"A high school teacher!" cried a third. The others turned to him in shock, but the crowd roared.

The actors presented skits that portrayed all the stereotypes people believed about one another: the drunken Irishman, the stingy Jew, the lazy black man, and the greasy Hispanic. Michael and his crew humorously pointed out that there was good and bad in every person. "Nobody's perfect, and nobody is like anybody else," Michael shouted. The cast got together for a final song called "Get to Know Me for Me."

A few students were humming the final tune as they left the auditorium.

"What did you think?" Julie asked Tasha as they headed for their lockers.

"I liked it," said Tasha. "I hope it helped."

When Sarah and Tasha went to 18 Pine St. that

afternoon, they found only April, Kwame, and Robert there. April looked as if she had been crying.

"Are you all right?" Sarah asked her.

"I'm fine, it's Steve I'm worried about," April replied. "He said he doesn't want to hang out here anymore because he doesn't want to keep defending whites to people. He said he feels like people are judging him."

"That's ridiculous," cried Tasha. "Nobody said anything about him."

April shook her head. "You didn't have to say anything. He feels guilty anyway."

"Speaking of guilty," Robert murmured. He pointed to the doorway of the pizzeria.

Sarah and the others looked up and saw Rick Hathaway standing by the door. When Rick spied the group, he made his way over.

"They told me I'd find you guys here," said Rick. He looked uncomfortable but determined. "I just want you to know I didn't write those marks on the wall, even though everybody thinks I did. I wouldn't do something like that."

Robert began to hum the melody to the song "Get to Know Me," and Tasha laughed.

"Yeah, it's all a big joke to you, Robert," said Rick softly. "But I don't hate you; I don't hate anybody."

"You can be prejudiced without hating someone," Kwame said sharply. "You just have to think less of them. Telling that joke proved you think less of us."

"I don't think less of you," said Rick. "I just think I have the right to say whatever I want! And you have the right to disagree with me."

"What about 'KKK'?" said Robert sarcastically. "Is that part of your free speech?"

"I didn't write that!" said Rick vehemently. "But it looks like you've all made up your minds about me. Now who's being prejudiced?" He stormed out of the pizza shop.

"I didn't want to say it in front of him," said April. "But he had a point."

"Oh, come on!" said Tasha. "He's just trying to sound sorry because his butt is in trouble over that 'KKK' thing. Maybe he *didn't* write it, but somebody did, and that makes me feel mad and threatened. If that's the way Rick feels, then good! Now he knows what it's like."

"Well, Steve hasn't done anything wrong, and he feels bad," April snapped. "Why does he feel like he's being punished? Is it because he's white?"

Nobody could answer her.

Twelve

If the teachers had counted on the assembly to ease tensions at Murphy High, they were soon disappointed. On Friday, Rick Hathaway got into a fight with Tyler McPeak, a black linebacker who said he was doing it on behalf of the black student body. There were plenty of people who saw Tyler pick the fight, so he was the only one who got suspended. When Rick arrived at Sarah's history class that day, he was holding an ice pack over his swollen eye.

"When is it going to stop?" Sarah said as she and Tasha rode the bus home.

Tasha pointed outside the window. "It hasn't stopped out there, so why should it stop at Murphy?" She turned to her cousin and lowered her voice. "I'm going to organize a sick day for next Wednesday. All the blacks, Hispanics, and everyone else who's sick of racism will stay out of school."

"Tasha, don't we have enough problems?" said Sarah. "That will just divide the school further, not bring it together."

Tasha laughed. "I swear, girl, sometimes I don't know whose side you're on."

Miss Essie was waiting for them when they got home. "She's home," she said. Sarah and Tasha saw a colorful "Welcome Home" banner strung across the banister that ran along the upstairs hallway. The Gordon cousins dropped their book bags and ran upstairs.

"You look great," Tasha said.

"It's good to have you back, Mom," said Sarah, wiping a tear from her eye. "How do you feel? Can I get you anything?"

"Who's been making all those tuna casseroles in the fridge, you or Tasha?"

The cousins laughed and explained about Mrs. Hunter and the well-meaning ladies of her church.

Sarah called Cindy to tell her about her mother's return. But Cindy had some news of her own.

"I almost bumped into the Mad Soaper!"

"What!" Sarah's shout brought Tasha to the hallway. Sarah frantically waved her cousin to the phone, and they both listened intently.

"I took the late bus home today because I had to talk to Ms. Sanchez about my Spanish grade—never mind what she told me about that! Anyway, we were both heading down that stairwell in the back of the building, and we heard footsteps running off. When we turned the corner, we saw huge letters that said 'Yo, Peace,' except the guy didn't have a chance to finish the final 'e,' so it reads 'Yo, Peace.'"

"Did you get a look at him?" Tasha asked.

"I didn't get a good look, but I saw him run through the double doors at the bottom of the steps. I saw the top of his head, and he was definitely black!"

"Who was it?" Sarah asked.

"I don't know," said Cindy. "But he was kind of short. About Kwame's height!"

Kwame flatly denied he was the Mad Soaper when he showed up at the Gordon home on Saturday morning. "It couldn't have been me because I was at the city library getting these out." He held up a stack of books. "They're books on debating and hate speech. We're going to be ready for Rick on Tuesday."

Tasha and Kwame spent the rest of Saturday working at the kitchen table. They had the books spread all around them. The coaching didn't go very well. "No *ad hominem* attacks," said Kwame, reading from a book on debating tactics.

"What the heck is that?" said Tasha.

"It means don't criticize the person you're debating, just the person's ideas."

Tasha gave him an impatient look. "I know all that," she said. "I don't think we should be looking in a book for this kind of stuff. I just want to talk about how I feel."

Kwame gave her a troubled look. "Rick Hathaway is

going to know all the debating tactics. You'd better learn them as well, or he will have an advantage over you."

"This argument isn't about debating tactics, it's about my right to go to high school without hearing things that demean me as a black person!"

"Maybe so," said Kwame. "But a debate isn't just a shouting match. You have to go by certain rules. You make your arguments, then he makes his. Then you respond to his points, and he responds to yours. And finally, you each sum up your argument one last time, and the judges decide who wins. So you can't just go up there and say what you feel."

"I know," said Tasha, taking the debating book out of his hands. "But what's important is *what* I want to say, not *how* I say it."

"They're both important," said Kwame stubbornly.

"Well, let's come back to the debating tactics later," said Tasha. But the rest of the afternoon flew by, and they became so engaged in Tasha's arguments that they never returned to the debating book.

On Sunday, Tasha dug out the phone list she had made for the kente cloth day, and told all her friends about Wednesday's Sick of Racism Day. At one point, she looked up from her dialing and found Sarah staring balefully at her.

"Call it off," Sarah told Tasha.

"I'm not going to call it off," Tasha replied. "We need it now more than ever."

"You'll just be stirring people up even more," said Sarah.

"People need to be stirred up," Tasha insisted.

"Haven't we had enough of that with Wayne getting into fights with Robert, and someone spraying 'KKK' on the school walls?" asked Sarah. She gave her cousin a knowing look. "If you ask me, I think you're enjoying the attention you're getting."

"This Sick Day is a chance for the minorities to do something together," said Tasha. She grinned. "But I gotta admit, it's nice to have freshmen and juniors coming up to me and telling me they're proud of me for challenging Rick. Steve Adams isn't the only one who's been surprised to find racism alive and well. If I'm speaking for the blacks in the school, I'm proud to do it."

Thirteen

On Monday morning, the day before the debate, Julie O'Connor rushed to Sarah's locker with the stunning news. "Did you hear about Rick Hathaway?" she said breathlessly. "He's been expelled!"

"What?" Sarah cried.

"I couldn't believe it, either," said Julie. "They found a pair of shoes in his gym locker that matched the footprint the police discovered by the wall. Of course, Rick says they aren't his shoes, but what else would he say, you know?"

Sarah couldn't believe it. Rick had looked sincere when he had talked to her friends at 18 Pine St. She was convinced he wasn't the culprit.

Kwame had his doubts as well. When the group met for lunch, he shook his head at the news. "I was sure it was Wayne," he said.

Mr. Cintron, who was monitoring the cafeteria that

afternoon, approached their table. "I'm afraid there won't be a debate tomorrow after all," he said. "Rick has been expelled from Murphy High."

"You mean suspended, don't you?" said Robert. He had a troubled look on his face.

Mr. Cintron shook his head. "No, I said 'expelled.' Writing 'KKK' on the wall is serious stuff, Robert." He surprised them by taking a seat at their table. "Kwame, you're the history expert. What is the KKK?"

"The letters stand for the Ku Klux Klan, which was a secret group started after the Civil War to scare the former slaves," said Kwame. "They covered their heads with white capes and went around the countryside terrorizing black people to keep them from voting, or getting too powerful."

"Exactly," said Mr. Cintron somberly. "What the KKK really wanted was to keep things the way they had been before the Civil War. They wanted to keep black people frightened and powerless, and they killed those who opposed them. Eventually, they aimed their hatred at other groups who threatened the old racist ways: Jews, Catholics, and immigrants."

"Shoot! If I know Rick, he'll say he was exercising his freedom of speech when he wrote on that wall," said Jennifer scornfully.

"No," said Mr. Cintron. "This isn't like telling a joke to one of his friends. First of all, he defaced school property, which is illegal. And second, those initials can only be taken one way—as an insult to minorities." He turned to Robert again. "He had to be expelled, Robert.

How would you like to go to Murphy High, knowing there was a boy who was loyal to a group that spouted hatred and intolerance?"

As Mr. Cintron was leaving the table, Sarah stole a glance at Robert, who had a faint sheen of sweat on his brow. "I thought you'd be happy to hear the news, Robert."

"Expelling him was going too far," said Robert. "I thought he'd be suspended for a while, not kicked out of school altogether."

Sarah could no longer contain the suspicious thought that had been forming inside her. "Robert, tell me the truth: did you write 'KKK' on the wall?" she asked.

Billy, Dave, and the others turned to her with shocked looks.

"Of course not!" Robert cried. "Why would you even think something like that?"

"Because your chin dropped about a hundred feet when you found out that Rick had been expelled," said Sarah. "And because you talked about giving Rick a taste of his own medicine at 18 Pine last week."

Kwame looked at Robert with a troubled expression. "When you dropped me off at home after the Battle of the Bands, you were talking about getting even," he said. "Did you go back to the school that night?"

Robert gave his friend a comical grin, but he was clearly nervous. "I'm not going to answer that, Your Honor," he said, imitating a man on trial.

"You don't have to answer it," said Billy. "Your face is giving you away. But I thought you were mad at Wayne.

111

Why did you put the shoes in Rick's gym locker instead?"

"Not so loud!" said Robert, glancing at a cluster of students who were eating near their table. "Because Rick is the real problem. He's the one who talks about free speech and his rights, and then dummies like Wayne come in and think they've got permission because of it."

"Well, you'll have to go to Mr. Schlesinger's office and tell him," said Jennifer.

"Are you nuts?" Robert cried. "If I come forward, then I'll be the one who gets expelled."

"And you'll deserve it!" said Sarah. "How could you frame an innocent person like that?"

"Sure, stick up for the white guy!" said Robert, rolling his eyes.

"Sarah is sticking up for what's right!" said Cindy. "What you did was terrible."

Robert looked around the table for support. But his friends looked back at him with disgust, especially Tasha. "You against me, too, Tasha?" he said.

"You went too far," said Tasha, standing up suddenly. "You gotta tell Mr. Schlesinger the truth."

Robert slammed his hand on the table. "No! Tasha, I did it for you. I'm sick of having white folks say nasty things and then pretend it's about freedom of speech. Why are people always 'free' to insult us? They never feel 'free' to make us feel good about ourselves. Kwame—you're Mr. Historian here—tell them," he said, gesturing to the others. "White folks in history have cheated on us, blamed us for things we didn't do, and stolen the credit for things we *did* do. They haven't played fair with us, why should we play fair with them?"

"That's not Rick's fault," said Kwame quietly.

"Yeah," said Dave. "He wouldn't do something like spray-paint letters on a wall. He has black friends, and—"

"So what?" said Robert angrily. "That doesn't mean a thing!"

Sarah and the others argued with Robert, trying to persuade him to turn himself in.

"I'm not going to Mr. Schlesinger's office," said Robert. "And if someone accuses me, I'll deny it. I'll tell Mr. Schlesinger someone is trying to frame *me*!"

Dave let out a harsh laugh. "Man, all Schlesinger has to do is ask your mom if those shoes you planted in Rick's locker are yours. When she says yes, you're done for."

"Wait, everybody," said Billy. "We can't let Robert turn himself in! We'll never be trusted after this. If something racist happens again, people will say, 'Oh, it was just a black student trying to frame someone.'"

"*Neither* side should be allowed to get away with it," said Tasha hotly. "The students need to know that the person who wrote this hate speech has been caught."

"No they don't, because I'll never do it again," said Robert. "You *know* that."

"What does that mean?" said Sarah. "That Rick takes the blame for something he didn't do? Maybe *you* can live with that, but I can't." She stood up and looked at Robert with a mixture of anger and pity. "I'm going to the main office. Are you coming with me?"

Robert took one last look at his friends, but found no sympathetic faces. "Traitors!" he said, near tears. He grabbed his book bag from the top of the table and stormed out into the courtyard toward the main office. Sarah and Tasha hurried after him.

Mr. Schlesinger was stunned when he heard Robert's confession. "This is terrible," he muttered. His glance fell on Tasha and Sarah. "Were you two part of this?"

"No!" the Gordon cousins chorused.

"We're here to back up our friend," said Tasha. She walked up to Robert, who sat on the vice principal's battered sofa. "I'm proud of you," she whispered.

Robert said nothing.

PINE

Fourteen

That afternoon, Sarah ran upstairs to tell her mother the news about Robert. She hurried up to her parents' bedroom, and walked in to find her mother tying a large silk handkerchief on her head. Mrs. Gordon looked thinner than Sarah had ever seen her. The minute Sarah noticed the handkerchief, tears began to form in her eyes. She had read about the side effects of the chemotherapy that followed many cancer operations. "Mom, did you lose your hair?"

"No," said Mrs. Gordon, smiling. "It's a little too early in the treatment for that. I just didn't have the time to comb it." She pulled off the kerchief and revealed a full head of hair. "See?"

Tears streamed down Sarah's cheeks. "But it *will* happen, won't it?"

"Perhaps. But it will grow back after I stop taking the pills," said her mother.

"How long do you have to take them?"

"Everyone responds differently to chemotherapy," said Mrs. Gordon, sitting down on the bed. "I'll know more when I go back to the hospital for more tests next week."

"More tests!" cried Sarah.

"Yes. And more tests after that," said Mrs. Gordon. "Treating cancer takes a long time."

Sarah headed back to her room, feeling depressed. When she walked past Tasha's bedroom, she overheard her cousin talking about the Sick of Racism Day. She waited at the doorway until her cousin hung up.

"You're still going to boycott school, even though it was Robert who spray-painted the letters?" Sarah asked.

"That's right," said Tasha. "Mr. Cintron canceled the debate we were going to have tomorrow, so we still need to do something to prove to everyone that we minorities are organized. Then they'll think twice about messing with us."

"Isn't there a better way to do it than skipping school? Couldn't we hold a rally at lunchtime or something?" said Sarah.

"I already told everyone to stay out of school on Wednesday," said Tasha. "I can't change it now." She gave her cousin a meaningful look. "What about you? Are you in with us, or out?"

Sarah hesitated. Deep down, she was proud of her cousin's efforts on behalf of the black students in school. But she couldn't see herself faking illness in light of her mother's real pain. It would feel like a cruel joke. "I'm out," she said finally.

On Tuesday, the Gordon cousins were surprised to wake up and find Mr. Gordon in the kitchen, offering to take them to school. As principal of Hamilton High, a school for students with learning problems, Mr. Gordon was usually gone by the time Sarah and Tasha headed for the bus.

"I heard a rumor from one of the administrators in my office yesterday," he told them as he drove through downtown Madison. "She was on the phone with Mr. Schlesinger's secretary, and found out that you two helped catch the 'KKK' vandal."

"We didn't tattle on Robert," said Tasha quickly. "We talked him into giving up."

"I know," said Mr. Gordon, "and I'm proud of you both. It was the right thing to do."

"Is Robert going to be expelled?" asked Sarah.

"I don't think so," said Mr. Gordon. "I know the Thorntons pretty well, so I called Mr. Schlesinger to find out more. He's going to suspend Robert for a while, but neither he nor Rick will be expelled."

"But Mr. Schlesinger was ready to expel Rick Hathaway," Tasha pointed out. "Why not Robert?"

"Robert's case is a bit unusual," said Mr. Gordon as he stopped the car in front of the school. "A black boy writing anti-black graffiti is a special case. Mr. Schlesinger wants Robert to attend some counseling sessions."

During homeroom that morning, Mr. Schlesinger made an unusual announcement: "It gives me great pleasure to inform you that the person who defaced the building with the initials of the Ku Klux Klan was caught. The school extends an apology to Rick Hathaway, who was unjustly accused of the act."

Sarah—and the rest of the school—waited for Mr. Schlesinger to name the culprit, but instead he moved on to other announcements.

At lunch that day, Mr. Cintron found Rick and Tasha in the cafeteria. "I guess I was too quick to cancel the debate yesterday," the social studies teacher admitted. "Can we reschedule it for tomorrow afternoon?"

Sarah looked at Tasha. Wednesday was her cousin's Sick of Racism Day.

"How about Thursday?" said Tasha innocently.

"Fine by me," said Rick. He hesitated a moment, then extended his hand to Tasha. "Good luck."

Tasha looked taken aback. "You, too," she managed to say.

Fifteen

On Wednesday morning, Sarah was not surprised to see Tasha walking into the kitchen in her nightshirt, complaining about a sore throat.

"You seemed fine last night," said Miss Essie, feeling Tasha's forehead.

Tasha gritted her teeth. "My stomach feels queasy, too," she said in a raspy voice.

When Miss Essie left the room to find a thermometer, Tasha gave her cousin a wink. "Last chance, Sarah," Tasha whispered. "If you go, you're going to be the only black person in school today."

A few other black students did show up that morning, among them Dave Hunter. But he and Sarah were the exceptions. Tasha's boycott had been remarkably effective. By the time Sarah went to math class, someone had tipped off the teachers about what was going on, and she could see a few them conferring in the hallways.

"I haven't seen Jennifer or Kwame," said Dave when he and Sarah met between classes that morning.

"Cindy, José, and Marc Halle are out 'sick,' too," said Sarah.

She counted eight empty chairs in her history classroom that afternoon. She was glad to see Rick Hathaway back in his usual seat.

"I'll have to tell Tasha her plan was a big success," Sarah told Dave when the final bell rang. They were surprised to hear Rick calling after them.

"I wanted you to show this to your cousin," said Rick in a voice tinged with weariness. "This is a copy of what I'm going to write in the next issue of *The Murphy Monthly*."

Sarah and Dave read the letter:

In the last issue, Tasha Gordon wrote a letter complaining about a joke I told. I didn't think it was offensive, but she did. I just want to publicly apologize to Tasha for any pain or humiliation I caused. I've gone through a lot of pain and humiliation myself. As the guy in the assembly said, "Get to Know Me," because I'm not the racist everyone thinks I am. I didn't write anything on Murphy's walls, and I don't know who did. I'm sorry everything got so out of hand.

It was signed simply "Rick." Sarah looked up from the note with a questioning glance.

"It's going to come out next Thursday, but I thought Tasha should know early so we can stop fighting."

"But what about the debate?"

"There isn't going to be a debate!" said Rick. "You can tell Tasha she won! Follow me," he said, motioning Dave and Sarah to his locker. Sarah noticed that his hand was trembling as he spun the combination lock fiercely. The smell of Kool-Aid hit her nostrils as he opened the door.

"Look at my jacket!" he said.

Rick's jacket hung inside the locker. Sarah and Dave immediately saw the large red stain on one of the sleeves.

"It happened this morning," he said. "I found this note next to it that said, 'Who's got a red suit now?'" He slammed the locker door and looked at Sarah tiredly. "It's over," he said simply.

"You can't give up," said Sarah. "You've got to debate her now more than ever."

Rick glared at her. "What for? Don't I have enough trouble already?"

"Sarah's right," said Dave. "The whole school is waiting for you and Tasha to square off so the whole issue can be settled once and for all." He gestured at the nearly empty hallways.

"I tried to make her understand it was not about my stupid joke," said Rick, shaking his head. "It's about the freedom to express yourself."

"If you really believe that, then you've got to fight," said Dave.

121

"Yes," said Sarah. "This is your only chance to defend your beliefs in front of everyone who wants to listen. You can't pass that up!"

"I guess not," said Rick dully. "I'm just tired of being *hated*."

"Feeling better?" Sarah asked her cousin when she got home.

"I made a miraculous recovery," said Tasha with a wink. She was dressed in faded jeans and a Georgetown sweatshirt. "In fact, I'll probably make it to school tomorrow."

"Good," said Sarah. "Because you're going to be debating Rick after school."

"I know," said Tasha. "I've been writing and rewriting my arguments all day. I'm ready for him!"

"Keep it down," said Miss Essie, appearing at Tasha's door. "Your aunt is trying to get some rest."

"I'm up, Miss Essie," said Mrs. Gordon, appearing at her side. She leaned heavily against the door frame. "This medicine makes me dizzy when I close my eyes. If you make me get in that bed, I'll go crazy!"

"We were talking about Tasha's debate tomorrow," Sarah told them.

"I'd love to hear your side of it, Tasha," said Mrs. Gordon.

"I was hoping you would!" said Tasha, "but you've been so tired, I didn't want to bother you with my—" A wave of emotion made her stop. She fought the urge to cry. "I've been so worried about you, Aunt Elizabeth! I

122

can't show it like Sarah, but please believe—!"

"I know," said Mrs. Gordon, approaching her niece and giving her a gentle embrace. "I know you care. We all show it in different ways."

Sarah found she was trembling with sobs herself. Miss Essie dug a tissue from the pocket of her housecoat and handed it to her, then took one for herself.

"Enough of this," said Mrs. Gordon firmly when Tasha had stopped crying. "Let's hear that debate!" She turned to Sarah and said, "Why don't you take Rick's position and we'll act the whole thing out."

"But I don't know what Rick is going to say!" said Sarah.

"He wants free speech, no matter what," said Tasha. "And I want free speech, but with responsibility."

Sarah ran to her bedroom and returned to Tasha's room with her desk chair to serve as a lectern. Tasha did the same with her chair. While she did this, Miss Essie took Mr. Gordon away from his plants in the basement to watch the proceedings.

"*Proposed*," said Mrs. Gordon in her most lawyerly tone. "*That the right to free speech cannot, and should not, be limited in any way.*" She pointed to Sarah. "You begin by defending the proposition, Sarah."

Sarah recited what she remembered of Rick's arguments, and was surprised at how much she recalled. Tasha made an impassioned speech about restraint and common sense. They traded the speaking role back and forth until Mrs. Gordon called for final comments.

When they were finished, Sarah was surprised to see

that her hands were shaking. Tasha had been a formidable opponent, but she thought she had held her own quite well. She looked at her parents and at Miss Essie, and found them beaming.

"You've got a great speech, Tasha," said Mrs. Gordon. "The only thing I want to warn you about is not to criticize Rick Hathaway personally. You called him a racist at one point. That's known as an *ad hominem* attack."

"Kwame warned me about that," Tasha muttered. She looked at the grown-ups and pointed to Sarah and herself. "Who won the debate?"

"Wait! I didn't get a chance to prepare the way you did," said Sarah. "I swear, cuz, you are too competitive for your own good!"

Mrs. Gordon smiled. "The biggest winner will be the audience that hears the real thing tomorrow."

Sixteen

Sarah and other members of the Ecology Club milled among the students who were gathering in the activities lounge for the big debate. The candy they had ordered to help raise money for the recycling bins had arrived, and they were doing a brisk business. Sarah had expected to see a good crowd in the lounge, but when the time came for the debate to begin, students were still filing in.

"Look at them all," said Sarah. She turned to her cousin. "Are you nervous?"

"A little," Tasha confided. She wore a tailored blue suit and a white blouse. It was the same outfit she wore to church on Sundays. Rick had also dressed up for the occasion. He wore a blue jacket, gray slacks, and a dotted yellow tie. His hair was still wet, and he looked every bit like the politician Sarah imagined he would become.

The number of chairs they had set up turned out to be too few, and the students began finding places on the floor, making life miserable for the Video Club members, who were trying to set up their equipment. The students continued to file in, finding seats on the tables that had been stacked in a corner.

"We're going to have to move somewhere else," Rick murmured to Tasha.

"Listen, people," Mr. Cintron yelled. "We're going to the auditorium. There's no room here." A wave of grumbling met this remark as students picked up their backpacks and books and headed for the door.

The auditorium wasn't filled as it had been for the racial awareness show the school had put on the week before, but Sarah was still astounded at the turnout. She counted one row of students and multiplied by fifteen and guessed that over three hundred students were attending.

It took some time for the microphones to be set up on the stage, and even more time for the lights to be turned on, but once everyone had sat down, Mr. Cintron explained the rules.

"Tasha Gordon and Rick Hathaway will debate the following proposition. 'Proposed: that the right to freedom of speech must include freedom of unwelcome speech.'"

Mr. Cintron guided Rick to a podium on the stage as he spoke. "Rick will begin by defending the proposition, then Tasha will make her argument against it. Rick will proceed with his *rebuttal*—which is just a fancy word for counterargument. Then Tasha will make her rebuttal of Rick's claims. Finally we will have closing arguments from each debater."

"Who's going to decide the winner?" shouted Brenda Greer from the audience.

"We will have three judges: Mr. Loving, Mrs. Parisi, and myself. Scores will be given for organization, strength of argument, and speaking skills."

Mr. Cintron motioned for Rick to begin, but before he could open his mouth, a small group of students began chanting in the back. "Racist! Racist! Racist!"

"Give him a chance," said Tasha into her microphone. "Let him say what he has to say."

When the noise in the crowd died down, Rick began.

"Free speech is a right that is guaranteed by the Constitution—even speech that we might find offensive. If we forbid certain words or ideas because we're afraid of offending someone, soon everyone will have something they don't want to hear. And what was once a country that was built on the belief that we could talk things out to find a common ground, will turn into a country that is too afraid of speaking at all." Rick finished his speech and sat down to polite applause.

"He started out pretty good," Cindy whispered to Sarah.

Before Sarah could agree, she heard more people coming into the auditorium and turned to see who they were. She was very surprised to find her father,

Mr. Schlesinger, Mr. Parrish, and others from the school board standing in the open doorway. They quickly found seats as Tasha began her speech.

"As my opponent stated, free speech is one of the cornerstones of our democracy. But when speech is used to attack a minority group like blacks, who have been attacked for four hundred years in this country, it's time to say 'enough'! Free speech is like a gun. We don't want to take that gun away, we just want you to stop taking aim at us!"

A roar erupted from the crowd, and Sarah felt a chill race up her spine. It was not the way Tasha had started her side of the debate the night before. Even Rick was taken aback by the force of her words. He shuffled his papers as the roar melted into applause and finally into silence.

"It is now Rick's turn to rebut Tasha's argument," said Mr. Cintron. This time, no one interrupted Rick when he began.

"Tasha called freedom of speech a gun," said Rick. "But I think it's more like a light. We may see things we don't want to see, but it's better than the darkness of censorship."

Rick sat down to silence. Sarah knew that the majority of the crowd was behind Tasha because they broke into cheers and applause when she rose to take the stand. She adjusted the microphone so that it was close to her mouth, and then stunned the crowd again.

"Nigger," said Tasha.

It was as if a bomb had gone off in the room. Even the teachers looked shocked. "Spic, Kike, Dago, Chink," Tasha continued. "These words have the power to make us feel small and ashamed of who we are. And they serve no useful purpose. Why is that speech protected? Society puts limits on other freedoms. Let's put a limit on the right of others to make us feel small!"

Again, Tasha sat down to whoops and cheers.

"Now we will hear the final arguments from each side," said Mr. Cintron. Rick will go first again."

"My conclusion will be brief," said Rick. "In 1861, many whites in the South did not want to hear the idea that blacks had a right to be free. For them, it was crude and hateful speech. We've changed a lot since then, but we're not done changing. So we must protect all speech, and not just what is fashionably 'good' right now."

"He's right about that," Sarah overheard a black freshman girl say.

When Tasha took to the podium for the last time, Sarah leaned forward apprehensively. She was worried about Tasha's closing argument. The night before, she had used her conclusion to make a personal attack on Rick Hathaway, and Mrs. Gordon had warned her against it. But to Sarah's surprise, Tasha had removed that part from her speech.

"My aunt was diagnosed with cancer two weeks ago," Tasha began. "The cancer has proved to be very difficult to get rid of. Hate speech is like that cancer. We've seen it divide our school, we've seen it weaken our school. And it's time to fight it!"

"That was great!" Cindy whispered to Sarah after the applause for Tasha had died down.

"Before we compile our scores, let's give both debaters a round of applause," said Mr. Cintron. "We'll be back in a few minutes."

"My mind is reeling," said Cindy as she and Sarah got out of their seats to stretch. "They both made such good points."

"I'd hate to be Mr. Cintron or the other judges," said Kwame, who had come up to them. "They've got their work cut out for them."

As if to prove Kwame's point, the teachers took a full ten minutes to return. In that period, the crowd began to chant, "Tasha! Tasha!"

Tasha crossed the stage and extended her hand to Rick. "You did great," she said.

"You did, too," said Rick, accepting the handshake. It felt natural to hug each other briefly, and they did. This prompted a series of catcalls and whistles from the crowd.

"The judges have come up with a winner," said Mr. Cintron. "And I hope this is not the last debate we hold like this." He looked at the paper in his hand. "The judges gave a score from one to five for each part of the debate: organization, strength of argument, and speaking skills. The maximum score is fifteen for each part. For speaking skills, the vote was Tasha: fifteen, Rick: fifteen. For strength of argument, Tasha: fifteen, Rick: fifteen. "Tasha's friends cheered." For organization, the vote was Tasha: thirteen, Rick: fourteen. The winner is Rick Hathaway by one point."

The smattering of applause was drowned out by a chorus of boos. Tasha felt stunned. Nevertheless, she managed to cross the stage again and gave Rick a second congratulatory hug.

Mr. Gordon walked down to the stage and gave Tasha a long hug. "I'm proud of you, honey. You did great."

"Thanks for coming to see me, Uncle Donald," said Tasha.

"I wouldn't have missed it for the world. It's just what the school needed to hear."

A woman who Tasha guessed was Rick's mother climbed onto the stage and hugged him fiercely. Rick smiled, but Tasha could see that his eyes were troubled. He moved away from his mother and approached Tasha again.

"You deserved to win," Rick told her.

"Thanks, Rick," said Tasha. "But the judges knew what they were doing."

After Kwame, Jennifer, Cindy, and the others had congratulated her, Sarah took her aside. "How do you feel, cuz?"

"It's just like losing a basketball game by one point," said Tasha. "When you were *that* close to winning, it seems to hurt a little more." She gave Sarah a wry smile. "I'll get over it."

Suddenly, Billy Simpson wedged himself between them. He picked up Tasha and turned her around. "I'm so proud of you, girl. I'm so proud! No wonder I never win an argument with you."

Tasha laughed. "I don't know why you bother trying," she said.

PINE

Seventeen

"A deal is a deal!" said Tasha.

"And I'm saying the deal is off!" said Rick. "You don't have to write that letter of apology in *The Murphy Monthly*."

"I'm not going back on my word," said Tasha.

The auditorium was nearly empty. Mr. Gordon had left to be with his wife, and most of Sarah and Tasha's friends had hurried off to catch the late bus home. Only Rick, Sarah, and Billy remained with Tasha.

"The school newspaper won't be coming out for another week," said Mr. Cintron when Tasha told him about the letter of apology. "But follow me. I think we can work something out."

He led Rick and Tasha to the computer room in his office, and Sarah and Billy followed them. With a flurry of keystrokes, he brought to the screen a copy of *The*

Murphy Monthly's masthead. "Write your letter on the screen, and we will put it out as an 'extra' edition."

"If she writes a letter," said Rick, "I want to write one, too."

Tasha wrote a straightforward apology in which she admitted that Rick was not racist.

Even though we don't see eye to eye on many things, I have to give him credit for sticking up for what he believes in.

What surprised her was Rick's letter. It took up the column next to Tasha's:

Unless you've been on the moon the past week, you probably know that two weeks ago I told a joke that some people found offensive, and I took a lot of flak for it. Since then, I've been defending my right to free speech, and I've taken a lot of flak for that, too. But after the debate last night I realized that just because I can say something, doesn't mean I should. I'm going to be a little more careful about what I say, especially if it is something that could bother a person as smart and as cool as Tasha. Murphy Rools!

Sarah looked at Rick with new admiration. The letter of apology he had shown her the day before had been written reluctantly. This one seemed to be written from the heart.

Mr. Cintron turned on the office copier and proceeded to run off over five hundred copies. "I will slip one into each locker before I go," he said.

"We'll help," said Tasha, pointing at Billy and herself. Sarah and Rick agreed to pitch in as well.

That was how they discovered the Mad Soaper.

Sarah came upon him first. She had just finished stuffing leaflets in the row of lockers that hugged the outside walls near the math office. She rounded the corner and nearly bumped into the young custodian whom she had seen washing the "Murphy Rools" lettering from the plate-glass windows of the cafeteria. He stood frozen to the spot with a huge cake of soap in his hand. The first three letters of "Murphy" were written on the tile floor.

"You!"

The custodian looked around in panic, then dropped the soap in the bucket of mop water he had next to him. He picked up the mop and began to wipe the letters away furiously. "It would be your word against mine," he said firmly. "I didn't write that 'KKK' on the wall," he said, suddenly frightened.

"I know," said Sarah. She was a little afraid, but she heard footsteps behind them, and was relieved to see Billy and Tasha rounding the hall from the other end.

Billy saw the lettering on the tile floor and immediately understood.

"I don't believe it," he muttered. Then he broke into a laugh. He laughed so hard, he found himself sliding to the floor, his back against the wall. Sarah, Tasha, and the young custodian looked at each other, worried.

"What are you people doing in the building at this hour?" said the young custodian, suddenly suspicious.

When Tasha told him they had permission to be there, his expression turned from angry to fearful again. Sarah noticed he was gripping the mop so tightly, his dark knuckles shone. The custodian began to mop the letters away.

"But why?" said Sarah.

"I don't know," the custodian said. "I guess I just liked to watch everyone get excited when a new message popped up. It was just more work for me, so I didn't hurt anyone by it." He gave them a quick smile.

"You drew a great Wally the goat," said Rick, referring to the school mascot.

The custodian seemed pleased. "I've been drawing since I was a kid—it's something I just got to do. And with soap and a wall, you can draw pretty big."

"Well, you fooled everybody, man," said Billy, shaking his head. "We called you the Mad Soaper! But don't worry, we won't tell anyone," he said. The others nodded in agreement.

"No, it's over," said the custodian, mopping the last of the letters off the floor. "It was a kick when nobody knew about it, but it wouldn't be the same now."

The custodian told them his name was Ray, and he was nineteen years old. He was married, and he showed them a picture of his wife and a baby named Aisha. Suddenly, Sarah felt a twinge of sorrow for him. He was just three years older than she was, but already he seemed much older.

"Maybe you're done drawing at Murphy," said Sarah. "But I hope you keep on drawing somewhere else. You have real talent."

"I draw cartoons off the TV for my little girl," said Ray. "From now on, I'll stick to that."

"Aisha Rools!" said Rick.

Eighteen

On Friday morning, Mr. Schlesinger led the announcements with news of the debate. "Those of you who were in the auditorium yesterday afternoon were treated to a fine exchange of ideas. For those who missed it, the Video Club has made a copy of it and it is available in the library. I strongly encourage you to see it. We're a community again," he said, sounding choked up.

After the announcements, Mr. Schlesinger read aloud a copy of *The Murphy Monthly* "extra" edition.

"Dang!" Tasha muttered. "If we knew he was going to do that, we wouldn't have had to print more than five hundred pages. What a waste of paper!"

"I didn't know you were interested in recycling again," said Sarah.

"I was always interested," said Tasha piously. "I just got a little sidetracked these past two weeks."

That afternoon in Mrs. Parisi's history class, the teacher embarrassed Rick by making him stand in the middle of the room to accept a round of applause for his effort in the debate. Then she embarrassed Sarah by asking her to represent her cousin as she led the class in applause again. "I'm going to show that debate to my freshman class next year," Mrs. Parisi told them.

The pizza shop was crowded with most of Sarah's friends that afternoon. Dave and Billy were busy handing out slices of the large pepperoni pizza that Mr. Harris had just placed on the table. Jennifer Wilson and Julie O'Connor were looking through a fashion magazine together. April and Cindy argued over which of the college boys sitting by the window was the cutest.

Even Robert Thornton was there. Although he had originally been suspended for five school days, Robert told his friends he would see them in school on Monday. "Mr. Schlesinger said I could serve out the rest of my punishment in detention hall if I kept going to the counselor." He gave them a smug expression and polished his nails on his shirt. "The fact is, Schlesinger can't run the school without me!"

"Sure," said Billy. "You got all that experience running your mouth!"

Everyone laughed, including Robert.

When Tasha appeared, Steve, Kwame, and José jokingly offered her napkins to autograph.

"I still think you were robbed, Tasha," Kwame told her. "You had that debate in your pocket."

"I thought so, too," said Steve Adams.

Tasha looked at him, surprised. "You were there, Steve?"

"Yeah," said Steve, blushing. "I wouldn't have missed it for the world."

Tasha could have soaked in her friends' admiration all afternoon, but she already had other things on her mind. She motioned for Billy to come closer. Tasha leaned in and whispered, "You're still taking me driving tonight, right?"

"Sure," said Billy.

Sarah sighed. "Some things don't change," she muttered to Cindy. But for the first time in a while, Sarah felt happy. She remembered the proud smile on her mother's face when she and Tasha had come home from the debate. She felt a sudden urge to call her mother and tell her all about Tasha's day of schoolwide celebrity.

"I'll be right back," she said. She gave Kwame a severe look. "Don't even *think* about eating my slice of pizza," she said.

Kwame gave her a hurt look and withdrew his hand from her plate. "You don't trust folks," he mumbled.

Sarah went to the pay phone and dialed home.

Miss Essie answered. "She isn't here, Sarah," her grandmother said. "Your father took her to the hospital for more tests."

Sarah's hand was trembling as she hung up. She closed her eyes and said a quick prayer for her mother's recovery. She made her way back to the table, thinking of all the things she wanted to tell her mother, and of all

141

the ways she wanted to make her proud.

Cindy noticed the stricken look on her friend's face, and the others did as well. "What's wrong, girl?" said Cindy.

"My mom is in the hospital again," she told them. Tasha cursed softly and leaned her head on Billy's shoulder.

"She'll make it through," Kwame declared, "just like she did before."

"That's right," said Cindy, rubbing Sarah's shoulder.

Sarah stared at the scarred table and blinked away the tears. "Thanks, but it's going to be a long time before she'll be well again."

"Until then, you've got us to back you up," said Dave. "All of us," he said, gesturing at the table. "Right, folks?"

Sarah looked up to see each friend raising a hand.

CHOOSE YOUR OWN ADVENTURE®

Horror–Mystery–Science Fiction–Sports
There are so many adventures to choose from!

- ❏ 0-553-27419-8 The Curse of the Haunted Mansion #5.....$3.25/3.99
- ❏ 0-553-29358-3 Ghost Train #120 ....$3.25/3.99
- ❏ 0-553-27053-2 Vampire Express #31 ....$2.99/3.50
- ❏ 0-553-56008-5 Horror House #140....................................$3.25/3.99
- ❏ 0-553-27453-8 Space and Beyond #4................................$3.25/3.99
- ❏ 0-553-28440-1 Through the Black Hole #97 ....$3.25/3.99
- ❏ 0-553-28482-7 Alien, Go Home #101................................$3.25/3.99
- ❏ 0-553-28837-7 Invaders from Within #110.......................$3.25/3.99
- ❏ 0-553-29303-6 The Forgotten Planet #133 ....$3.25/3.99
- ❏ 0-553-56007-7 Dinosaur Island #138................................$3.25/3.99
- ❏ 0-553-56004-2 Scene of the Crime #137 ....$3.25/3.99
- ❏ 0-553-28898-9 Skateboard Champion #112 ....$3.25/3.99
- ❏ 0-553-28795-8 Daredevil Park #114..................................$3.25/3.99
- ❏ 0-553-29294-3 Superbike #124..$3.25/3.99
- ❏ 0-553-29304-4 The Luckiest Day of Your Life #132 ....$3.25/3.99
- ❏ 0-553-29401-6 Behind the Wheel #121 ....$3.25/3.99
- ❏ 0-553-28202-6 Master of Karate #108...............................$3.25/3.99
- ❏ 0-553-56006-9 Roller Star #136...$3.25/3.99
- ❏ 0-553-56002-6 Motorcross Mania #139 ....$3.25/3.99

U.S./Can.

- -

Bantam Doubleday Dell, Dept. BFYR 13,
2451 South Wolf Road, Des Plaines, IL 60018

Please send me the items I've checked above. I'm enclosing
$_____ (please add $2.50 to cover postage and handling).
Send check or money order, no cash or C.O.D.s please.

Mr./Ms. _____
Name

_____
Address

_____
City   **State**   **Zip**

BFYR 13 11/93

Please allow four to six weeks for delivery.
Prices and availability subject to change without notice

CHOOSE YOUR OWN ADVENTURE ®